Break Fast at Bradgate

by

D.A. Ramsey

V·O·L·C·A·N·O PUBLISHING

Volcano Publishing,
13 Little Lunnon,
Dunton Bassett,
Leicestershire,
LE17 5JR

© D.A. Ramsey 1996

Typeset in 11 pt Times

This booklet is sold subject to the condition
that it shall not, by way of trade or otherwise, be lent,
re-sold, hired out, or otherwise circulated without
the publishers' prior consent.

All rights reserved. No part of this publication may be
reproduced or transmitted in any form or by any means,
electronic or mechanical, including photography, recording
or any information retrieval system, without permission in writing
from the publishers.

ISBN 1 898884 09 9

Acknowledgements

To John Hodgson, National Trust Archivist at the John Rylands Research Institute, University of Manchester for drawing my attention to many interesting items in the Dunham Massey Papers and for producing an excellent catalogue of the papers.
    Thankfully John alerted the Leicestershire Records Office to the fact that within the collection of documents there had been a very interesting and fortunate survivor, a household account book for Bradgate House covering the period 1678-81(EGR 12/2 - JR ref no) This was subsequently copied onto microfiche and purchased by the Leicestershire Records Office and catalogued as MF493 (128 frames). This purchase saved me frequent trips to Manchester to view my primary source material for which I am eternally grateful.

To The National Trust for depositing the Dunham Massey papers and allowing unrestricted access for research purposes.

To Tony Squires – my thanks once again for making photographs and maps from his own collection freely available to me.

To Peter Eccles for his work on the types of casks at short notice.

To Gerald Baker of Volcano Publishing for taking on the Bradgate series with 'Nowt taken out' and having the vision to see that all five books in the series will compliment each other.

Lastly to my wife Gloria, a sincere thank you for proof reading and correcting text and photograph captions.

Break Fast at Bradgate

Contents

Introduction .... (i)

An Insight 1

Purchases A–Z 21

Glossary of 17th century terms 29

Account Book – June 27th 1681 38

Bradgate House 1500-1739 41

Abandonment of Bradgate House 73

References 74

Ashby Castle 76

Weekly Accounts 78

Index 92

Break Fast at Bradgate

Illustrations

Aerial photograph of ruins	(ii)
Ruins of House in 1988	(iii)
House plan of c.1500	(iv)
Charlecote House	14
Bradgate House c.1746	15
Glasses	16
Bottles	17
Kitchens	18
Elizabethan Kitchen	19
Peacock and Deer	20
Sketch of Bradgate House kitchen	28
Brewhouse vats	36
Brewhouse at Charlecote House	37
Dovecote and Beehive	40
Casks and Barrels	43
Painting showing typical food of the time	53
Isinglass	57
Rent Day Dinner	73

The kitchen was just one of the many departments of a great house involved in catering for a large household.

Introduction

The contents of this book are based on the household/kitchen accounts recorded at Bradgate House, Leicestershire, during the three years 1679, 1680 and 1681.

As Bradgate House has been in ruins since 1740, it has been necessary to find engravings, photographs and postcards from similar houses to illustrate a number of items which are referred to in the main text.

Charlecote House, Warwickshire (National Trust) is an existing building having external features and outbuildings similar to those which would have featured at Bradgate House. The laundry room and brewing arrangements at Charlecote are particularly enlightening when viewed alongside the Bradgate accounts.

The 'Purchases A–Z, Bradgate House 1679–1681' are from primary source materials.

A glossary of 17th century terms is included to give insight and further information on items referred to in the main text.

The 'Value of Remains in the House' is the actual record of food and drink held at Bradgate on the stocktaking day of June 27th 1681.

Where more is known about the food and drink and sundry items referred to in the text, further amplification is given towards the rear of this book.

David A. Ramsey,
11th July 1996

Break Fast at Bradgate

An aerial photograph of Bradgate House looking east, taken by T. Squires in Spring 1985. The road from Groby leads in from the right (over bridge) and was formerly the main route from Bradgate to Groby. A cross wall (dotted line) ensured goods, provisions and visitors came to the house via Groby Gate (south) or Causeway Lane (Cropston) to the east.

Break Fast at Bradgate

Bradgate House ruins in 1988.
This view of the west wall of Bradgate House is probably the most recognisable face of the ruins for 20th century visitors. During the 16th and 17th centuries few, if any, visitors saw this side of the house. The reason being that the access road to Newtown Linford was not built, and visitors were expected to approach Bradgate House from the south (Groby and Ratby) or east (Cropston).

(iii)

Break Fast at Bradgate

Bradgate House around 1500
This plan will help identify those parts of the house mentioned in the following text.

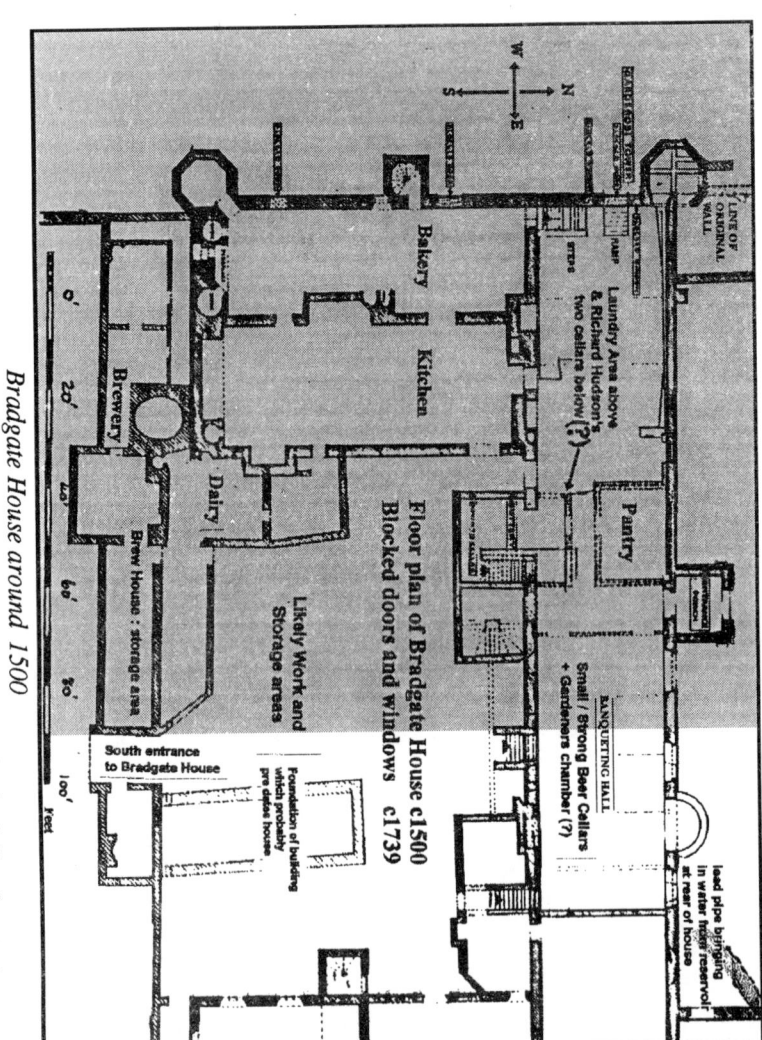

(iv)

Break Fast at Bradgate

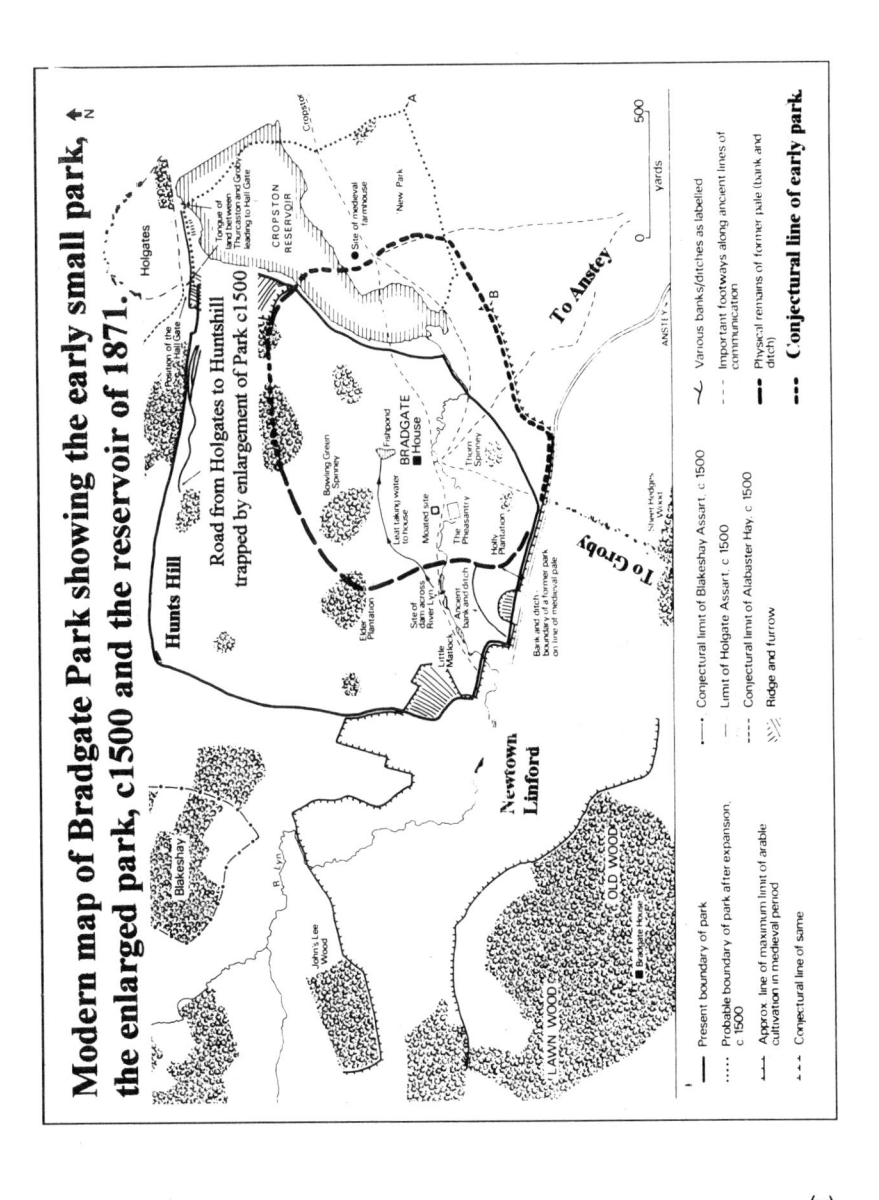

The earliest map of Bradgate Park and House c.1746

Although built as an unfortified building Bradgate House, standing in 800 acres of surrounding Park land, was originally not open to the casual caller. The Park, during the time the house was occupied between c.1500-1739, was deliberately managed so that it offered no entrances where deer could easily escape, allow a curious villager to get near the house, or even armed group to venture in without challenge. Towards the west (Newtown Linford) and the north sides there were small gateways in the walls surrounding the house.

These narrow gateways led into the rear of Bradgate House and enabled house staff to take barrels and bottles of ale and wine directly to the cellars. The house staff used horses kept in the paddock to the rear of the house to visit markets and the kitchen staff were also able to reach the cows and hens feeding close to the house through the same gateways. These entrances were for staff use only. The main entrance to the house was the eastern entrance – a carriageway lined by an avenue of trees. This avenue extended well beyond the deer barns (built in 1820) which today stand in the centre of the park and eventually joined with Causeway Lane, Cropston. A gate house, which still stands, stopped all traffic at the Causeway Lane entrance. To the south stood a lodge house which monitored all the Groby and Ratby traffic. This lodge house stood on the site of what is now the stone quarry, south of Bradgate House and just beyond the small bridge spanning the river Lin.

The map c.1746 on page 15 is well worth a few minutes study so that the walls and fences within the Park can be appreciated and the clever containment of both animals and people during the time of the occupation of the house can be noted.

An Insight into the Domestic Life at Bradgate House during the period 1679 and 1681

The surviving 17th century accounts for Bradgate House, near Newtown Linford, Leicestershire, reveal a regular timetable of events, spread over three years, as the goods and services received each week are methodically noted and paid for by Richard Frost, Steward of the Kitchen. There are obviously plentiful supplies of certain foods which have been purchased at local markets throughout the year. Then there are additional notes concerning the buying at Stourbridge Fair of salt fish, sugar and soap in much larger quantities. The latter event is a notable feature of the accounts as autumn begins. Sometimes it is possible to trace that salted sea fish, cockles and shore feeding birds have been purchased from as far away as the east coast. Fresh meats and fish are seemingly preferred but there always appears to be a plentiful supply of salted meat and fish, in hand, for use within the Bradgate kitchen when the normal fresh food supplies were either difficult to find, or just unobtainable due to the season of the year. The strict observance of keeping the fast days of Wednesday, Friday and Saturday would require that fish, in any form, rather than meat was always available, and in some quantity if necessary.

There were approximately 27 permanent domestic staff employed at Bradgate House during the late 1670s and early 1680s. At the height of the hay making, July/August, or the fruit picking season in early October, or when visitors were expected, extra casual staff were taken on. Luke Grocock the gardener in charge of just over 22 acres of walled gardens at Bradgate had to perform his duties with the help of casual male and female day labourers, no full time helpers. This assistance with the digging, carting, lifting of vegetables, tying of branches in fruit fans and tidying was also not continuous, for the same men and women were called upon to undertake other diverse tasks within the park. The payments for these services and various other labours have been recorded as well as the

Domestic Life during 1679 and 1681

tools and materials used in and around the house. Female labour helping with the routine tasks of laundry and weeding is also far from regular. Indications of extra staff being employed can be found by observing the normal disbursements over a period of two years, noting the additional payments as, and when, these have been added. Extraordinary payments were noted in a little more detail and shown as additions to the more regular weekly payments for services or purchases of foods, wines, spirits, beers, ales etc.

The annual excursion for some of the Bradgate kitchen staff to Stourbridge Fair in September must have been much enjoyed by those lucky enough to attend. The fair site (now a suburb of Cambridge) was where the staff bought most of the soap by the firkin (approximately one third the size of a barrel) at the keenest of prices. The staff would also purchase various grades of coarse and fine sugar by the hundredweight. The accounts show that sometimes the combined weight of all these purchases would amount to over 20 hundredweight and a carter would have to be hired afterwards to carry the goods back to Leicestershire.

The end of September and beginning of October brought employment for at least ten extra hands to help with the careful picking and treading of crab apples, the bottling of small amounts of cider and the casking of larger quantities.

Verjuice, a kind of vinegar, was also made from crab apples at Bradgate. As soon as the crab kernels turned black the apples were taken to a trough and crushed with heavy wooden mallets called 'beetles'. The resultant mash was then scooped into a coarse hair cloth bag and pressed until all the liquid had run off into hogsheads. Verjuice is really a sharp cider and not a vinegar, although it was used in large quantities for pickling by those in charge of the Bradgate kitchen during the 17th century.

Domestic Life during 1679 and 1681

By the late 17th century beer was being brewed at Bradgate as well as ale. Beer had been slow to gain favour in many parts of Britain and in the north and west the bitter flavour of the hops was not liked at all. Strong beer stocks in June 1681 were held in both casks(hogsheads) and bottles. The 23+ hogsheads alone – 52+ gallons in each hogshead – represent a substantial 1234 gallons and a further 270 bottles of strong beer – approximately 25 gallons – were held in one cellar as the stock check took place. A further 86 bottles were held in another cellar. Yet the same week's cash outgoings show that a further 22 bottles of strong beer had been purchased. Such was the strength of strong beer at this time that the beer glasses held approximately 3 to 4 ozs. of liquid, far less than a quarter of a pint.

The topping-up of beer and ale stocks at Bradgate appears to continue almost without reference to the large stocks of both already in hand in the cellars, or even the time of year.

Traditionally the new brewing began during late September or early October. The hops were delivered and then staff, skills, strength and knowledge, gained from previous brewing sessions were brought together once more. One really good brew of ale could be split and have varying quantities of twenty or thirty herbs or spices like rosemary, cinnamon and pepper added. This achieved high acclaim for anyone giving a banquet, for to friends and guests it would appear that their host was a man able to keep a quite remarkable range of ales in a quite modest cellar.

The long winter months brought with them a scarceness of fresh meat. Salted fish, oysters and cockles were all available but decidedly devoid of the delicate subtle tastes associated with the freshly caught foods. During these months, a larger number, and greater diversity, of birds were sought and purchased by the Bradgate kitchens. Pigeons were always available on site, in fact there are references to repairs to the Bradgate dovecot as late as 1787, long

Domestic Life during 1679 and 1681

after the abandonment of the house which had taken place in the autumn of 1739. Fieldfares, larks, geese, ducks, teal, wigeon, turkey, wood hens, partridge, pheasant and woodcock were just a few of the birds prepared by the Bradgate kitchens.

Birds had a two-fold appeal, firstly as supplies of fresh meat, especially during January, February and March, when travelling to Loughborough, Hinckley and Leicester markets became difficult due to the poor state of the roads, or ice and snow prevented all but the most parochial of movement. Secondly, because of their varied species, a difference in taste and meat texture could be offered to those dining. The dinners of the nobility and gentry, who often entertained guests, were normally served in two main courses, each made up very largely of meat dishes. Menus which have survived show it was rare for the meat of any type of animal to appear more than once in a course, or indeed in a meal. By serving birds in all their diversity, it was possible to avoid any hint of repetition.

When fresh water fish stocks were low a group of men and boys would be quickly assembled and dispatched to Groby Pool, or to the waters around the three mills at Thurmaston which in the 17th and 18th centuries were part of the Earl of Stamford's Leicestershire estates.

Vegetables were grown within the walled gardens on the north eastern side of Bradgate House. The accounts give one or two references to the buying in of vegetables such as artichokes and potatoes at this time. With the house having such large gardens it is perhaps not surprising to find that nearly all the vegetables required by the cook were available from the gardener. The accounts present a picture of a house buying in large quantities of meat, fish and drink, over and above the normal estate supplies. Some of the foodstuffs came into the house in the form of rent in kind, or as was the case

Domestic Life during 1679 and 1681

with butter was made by local farms. Vegetables are rarely mentioned yet their presence is inferred. There are additional notes within the accounts which mention the purchase of nets to carry cabbages and the buying in of mustard, radish and onion seeds. The vegetable garden at Bradgate would appear therefore to have been able to supply most of the cooks requirements. This self-sufficiency makes things difficult for the historian, for as there was no need to produce lists of payments made for vegetables, the few clues that are available give only a few indications as to what was actually grown in the vegetable gardens. Flaskets – shallow baskets for carrying produce, both for the gardener and dairy maid are mentioned, as is the frequent extra local help recruited to dig, fetch and carry in the twenty-two acres of house gardens and beyond.

Bradgate House kept cows, poultry, pigs and sheep close by. This early form of animal management system was later to develop into a completely detached 'home farm' in most parts of Britain but still serving the main needs of the near, or adjacent house. The 'home farm' would feature widely in the organisation of later 18th and 19th century manor houses and mansions; long after the abandonment of Bradgate House (1739) itself. 17th century Bradgate's animals were attended by the kitchen staff and dairy maid, with some outside help from the ever available casual labour force, the majority of whom were drawn in the main from the estate tenant families of Newtown Linford and Anstey.

A few animals are mentioned when oats are drawn for feeding the 6 coach mares, the keepers' 4 horses, 2 small running horses for swift journeys, and the staff bay (reddish-brown) horse – which was in daily use in view of the number of times it received new shoes. The bay would have been used for less strenuous errands and excursions in the local area.

Domestic Life during 1679 and 1681

Estate partridges, pigeons, pullets, swine and even the swans on Groby Pool also received their weekly supply of oats depending on the season.

Oatmeal was prepared for the dogs and the three liners which fitted into the dogs feed troughs are replaced during the period covered by the account book. The accounts also record that the sheep were washed and clipped (July) and the swine were ringed in December, the wire necessary for this task being purchased well before the actual ringing.

It seems likely that the house sheep and cows were contained in an area both south and west of the house. Towards the south, Dog Kenell (sic) Meadow was a largely fenced area. On the western side of the house, Spinny Laund contained the animals reasonably close to the pheasantry, this walled enclosure still exists, close to the modern tarmacadamed routeway through the park. The small amount of available grazing land not thoroughly over run with bracken could be sectioned by using portable hurdles and this would have ensured that the dairy maids did not have to search needlessly for the cows and at the same time the small amount of grazing available close to the house could be sectioned and grazed in a systematic way. In *The History and Antiquities of the County of Leicester*, Nichols includes an engraved plate of cows both standing and lying with calves in a field towards the west of the house with no bracken or fern in sight, yet it is quite obvious from the hasty bricking up of the house windows and doorways as the house was abandoned in the autumn of 1739 that good grassland was at an absolute premium anywhere within the park and the scene shown by Nichols's engraver is a highly subjective one.

Seeing that there was adequate water for the sheep and cows would have been an added chore, for the water course towards the

Domestic Life during 1679 and 1681

north western corner of the house carried drinking water and was fenced to keep out cows, deer and sheep. The river Lyn ran in front of the house but did not offer the type, or quantity, of grazing ground close to its banks, which could be constantly grazed. Added to this was the close restrictive proximity of both the Groby Lodge – now a quarry site south of the house – astride the bridle road, from Bradgate House to Groby, immediately south-west of the house – and the dog kennels for the hounds due south of the house.

The actual size of the Bradgate sheep flock appears to have been between 40 and 60 head during the 1679 to 1681 period rising to approximately 100 head. After the house had been vacated and abandoned, the walls were secured and windows bricked up; the sheep numbers rose to 120+. The house grounds and walled gardens were secured by bricking up all the cellar and ground floor level windows and doorways in the autumn of 1739.

The dairy maids c.1680 would have milked the cows by taking their stools and pails to the animals in the park. (The age old practice of taking a milking stool to the animals being milked was noted and commented on by William Martin, the Earl of Stamford's estate agent in 1845 – almost two centuries later. The practice was stopped shortly after William Martin's death in 1847).

Additional laundry assistance, on a casual basis, is rarely noted in the accounts. This is due to the fact that two laundry maids were already part of the Bradgate house staff and visitors, or 'strangers', as they are referred to were few in number. The modest laundry requirements may of course be due to the fact that only when the Earl of Stamford and his wife were in residence, and receiving visitors, was extra laundry help required. Normally the Earl and Countess of Stamford divided their time between their London house and their considerable estates in Cheshire, Leicestershire, Nottinghamshire and Staffordshire.

Domestic Life during 1679 and 1681

The account book mentions a game larder, a Butler's pantry, Butlers room and kitchen boys quarters but the exact location of these rooms remain unknown. It is thought that the kitchen boy's quarters – two are mentioned – would most likely have been above the kitchen.

Permanent Staff at Bradgate 1678 - 1681 **	Likely Position
Mr Slippen	Butler(?)
?	Butlers boy/coach boy
?	Chamber maid
John Burrows	Chaplain at Bradgate*
?	Coachman*
?	Cook*
?	Dairy maid(1)*
?	Dairy Maid(2)
Mr Godfrey	Footman(?)
Luke Grococke	Gardener*(1)
Stephen ?	Groom (head)*
? ?	Groom (assistant)*
Leonard Kirk	Kitchen boy*
? Dingley	Kitchen boy*
? ?	Kitchen maid.
Miss Groves	My Lady's maid(?)
Suzanna Carr (hired 28.08.1679)	Scullery maid*(3)
Anne Poole (retires 09.1679)	Scullery maid*
Thomas Yearby	Servant*
Will Rogers (died 26.07.1679)	Servant*
Mr Becher	Steward of the House.

Domestic Life during 1679 and 1681

Richard Frost	Steward of the Kitchen
Thomas (a negro)	Page/coach boy
Richard Hudson	Pantry (Head of) + Cellarer*
Ruth Hudson	Pantry servant *[2]?
?	Park keeper
?	Parker's man
?	Postillion

Known wages:-
  (1) Luke Grococke was hired 26.07.1679 @ £ 12 0 0 per year.
  (2) Ruth Hudson   was hired 12.11.1679 @ £ 5 0 0 per year.
  (3) Susanna Carr   was hired 26.08.1679 @ £ 2 10 0 per year.
* Confirmed staff positions.
** Compare with Ashby Castle staffing in the year 1609 rear of this book.

Casual workers and services: (1679-1681)

Mr	Woods	Brazier
John	Rower	Brewing
Joan	Doer*	Brewing
Harry	Ansty	Brewing (helper)
John	Brown	Brewing (helper)
William	Ison	Brewing (helper)
Mr	Hood	Candle and Tallow chandler
William	Johnson	Carpenter.
Henry	Johnson (son)	Carpenter.
John	Ansty	Carter
Mr	Bass (of Leicester)	Carting.
Thomas	Cooper	Coopering
John	Biggins	Fisherman (Groby Pool)
Thomas	Shaw	Fisherman (Groby Pool)

Domestic Life during 1679 and 1681

Jacob	Litlin	Gardening
John	Rowe	Gardening
Thomas	Sly	Hay makers
Robert	Glover	Hay making & carrying
Robert	Allen	Hay carrier
Mr	Page (of Leicester)	Killing rats and mice
Widow	Dingley	Kitchen assistant
Ralph	Allen	Mault (fetching from Loughborough)
Edward	Pole	Mault (making)
Robert	Wheatly	Miller (Mill house)
Thomas	Glover	Nets (mending)
Thomas	Walker	Ricking hay
Thomas	Fletcher	Ricking hay
Thomas	Loake	Thatching the stacks
Thomas	Shaw	Ringing the swine
Mr	Brookesby	Sugar and spice
Mr	Freeman	Sugar etc
Aron	Mottley	Supplying locks
Mr	Cradock	Wine and ale

The services of a carpenter, when needed, were usually met by sending a message to the father and son team of William and Henry Johnson who resided in Main Street, Newtown Linford.

* A likely mis-spelling of 'Rower'.

Domestic Life during 1679 and 1681

Descendants of the Johnson family still live on Main Street in the Newtown Linford village. The family farm being situated opposite the hollow way, which until 1780 led directly into the Forest of Charnwood. This farm may well have been managed and owned by the family since the early sixteenth century and very probably for a lengthy period before this. John Johnson of Newtown is recorded in the Leicester Castle Quarter Sessions returns of 1608 which show victuallers and alehouse keepers for that year.

The nails which appear in the household accounts – One thousand four penny nails @ 2/10 – were not bought for the carpenters, for as carpenters were never actually on the permanent staff of the house, these nails would have been for use in the garden. The gardener, or his assistants, would loosely wrap strips of leather around fruit trees and bushes so that their branches might be nailed espalier fashion onto a wooden frame, or shaped in the form of a fan directly onto the brick walls which surround the orchard on the south side of the house.

Today the remains of the main fabric of Bradgate House give few indications of the activities carried out there by the servants previously mentioned. There are however a few obvious signs such as the cellars and the brewing area at the south-western corner of the house. The wide drain, also in the southwestern corner, would mean that the laundry room and wash house must also have been located close by to make use of this same feature.

The actual physical labour involved in the movement of water and coals from various holding points within the house and grounds at this time would have been very demanding indeed. It is known that part of the house was served with water from a lead cistern, weighing just over fifteen tons, but the whereabouts of this water tank is unclear due to the entry merely noting the weight of scrap lead.

Domestic Life during 1679 and 1681

Speculation as to the whereabouts of the various routeways out of and into Bradgate House have led to a number of misconceptions as to how the house was entered. Fortunately the survival of the Nicholas Kiddiar map marked with the date 1746 has proved beyond doubt that there never was a north entrance of any importance for the Grey family visitors, although this entrance was often used by the domestic staff to reach the fish ponds and paddock at the rear of the main buildings. The bay horse much used by the staff was probably quartered in this convenient paddock.

The main entrance to the house lay on the eastern side of the main house. A grand avenue of trees led up to the formal gardens which were enclosed by brick and Charnwood stone walling. Kiddiar's map shows the house and park as it was immediately prior to its abandonment in 1739, emphasising the grand tree lined avenue to the full. It was along this routeway that William III travelled with his considerable entourage when he visited Lord Stamford in 1696. Although the avenue terminates on Kiddiar's map close to where the Deer Barns stand today the road continued in a near straight line to become Causeway Lane, Cropston.

This routeway appears to follow the original Broadgate, where 'gate' means street and the ancient 'Broadstreet', followed the dry, high ground, from the direction of Cossington through Rothley, Bradgate, Markfield and onwards towards Ashby and even further west. Bradgate Park when first enclosed caused this routeway to divert towards the south passing alongside the parks south eastern ditch and pale prior to the perimeter walls being built. One strip of field alongside the park wall and close to the road between Anstey and Newtown Linford was still being called by the name 'The Broadgate' when the W.I. conducted their field name survey in 1970s.

Groby Gate – the entrance is passed by the later diverted 'Broadgate' as it reaches the B5327 road between Anstey and

Domestic Life during 1679 and 1681

Newtown – was the link between Bradgate House and the former residence of the Greys at Groby, Groby Old Hall. The Old Hall being the home of the Ferrers family until William Ferrers died in 1445. The Manor of Groby together with Bradgate Park was inherited by the Grey family in 1446.

Once Bradgate House was completed in the early 16th century (no one as yet has found documents which fix a building date) the Marquis of Stamford and the Countess moved from their rather dated buildings at Groby Old Hall into the more spacious surroundings to be found in Bradgate Park. The Manor Court however, continued to meet at Groby Old Hall twice yearly, and proceedings were never transferred to Bradgate House. The Old Hall in fact continued to be used for estate business well into the 19th century in spite of the building being declared 'ruinous' several times by the estate steward in the early 17th century. The two courts which met on 25th March (Lady Day, or Feast of the Annunciation) and Michaelmas (September 29th) each year also coincided with the twice yearly rent collections and rent dinners. Short term lettings of the Hall to yeoman farmers appear to be established by 1679 when Mr. Martin of Anstey is granted the letting for one year, along with a piece of ground known as the Orchard (rear of Hall) and Dowry (a granite hill towards Groby Pool, now the miniature rifle range as the hill was quarried away in the early 1900s) for one year at the rent of £15 0 0. Additional clauses in the letting asked that 'no land was to be ploughed, a horse, or mare, was to be provided for use of the court officials, and meals were to be provided for those attending the two courts held at the Old Hall during the year'.

Domestic Life during 1679 and 1681

When William Martin, the Leicestershire estate agent, died in 1847 after some forty years service to the Earl of Stamford the estate was for a short time in the hands of a Colonel Wildman. He was the appointed guardian for the Earl's estates and in turn he appointed Loftus Lunds, a briefless barrister as agent for life at £1000. Loftus Lunds demanded the Estate books and papers in spite of being told that the books were kept in duplicate and he also stopped the free joisting of tenants cows within Bradgate Park. In so doing the practice of milking cows twice a day in the park came to an end.

(The unpublished notes of Charles Martin written in 1879).

Charlecote House, Warwickshire – (National Trust)
The lead capped towers flanking left and right of the main house may originally have had cisterns inside them to collect rain water. This illustration is probably the closest to how Bradgate House may have looked in the 16th century.

Break Fast at Bradgate

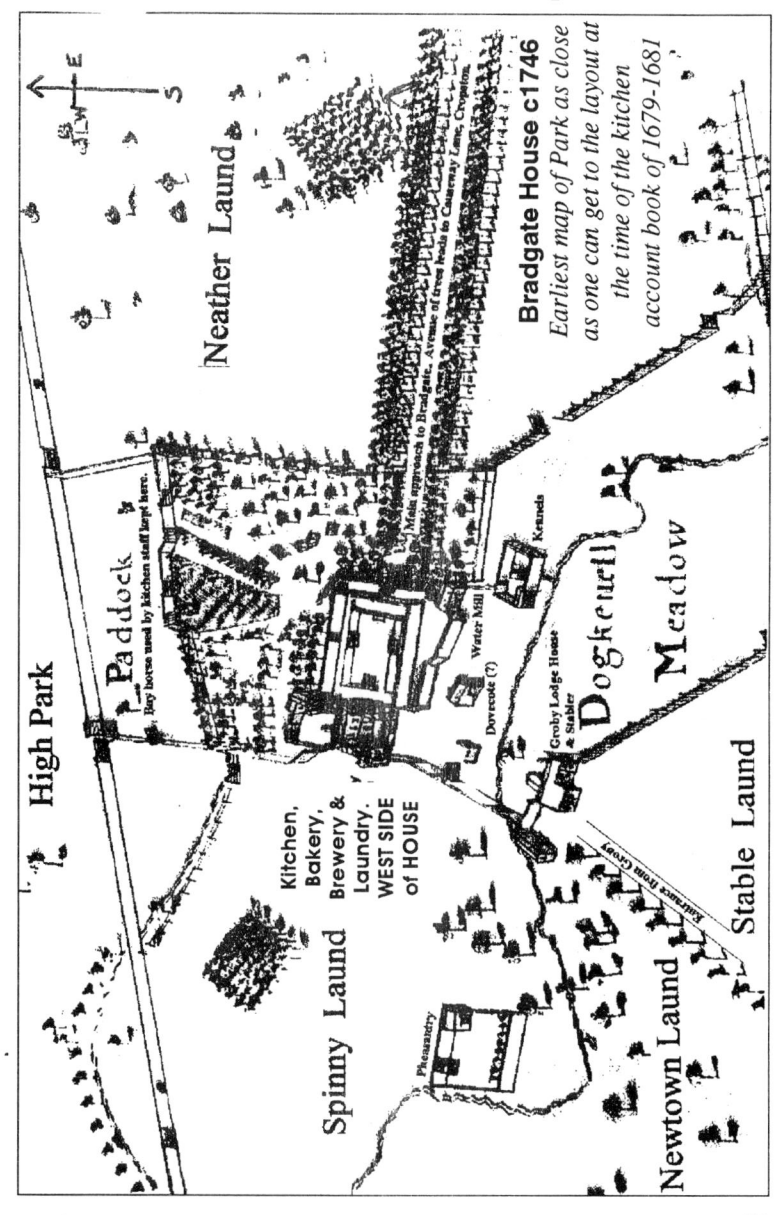

Bradgate House c1746
Earliest map of Park as close as one can get to the layout at the time of the kitchen account book of 1679-1681

Break Fast at Bradgate

Sweetmeats or suckets made from fruit preserved with sugar formed a most important part of a meal.

The colours and modelled shapes reflected the skills of the still-room staff.

Marmalades in particular were shaped into oak leaves and small fruit shapes.

A wine glass similar in style to the 3 dozen held in the Bradgate House pantry c.1680.

Ale glass c.1680. Small glasses were used at this time due to the strength of 'strong beer'.

Dry sweetmeats were placed in smaller glasses than the wet suckets, c.1680,

Break Fast at Bradgate

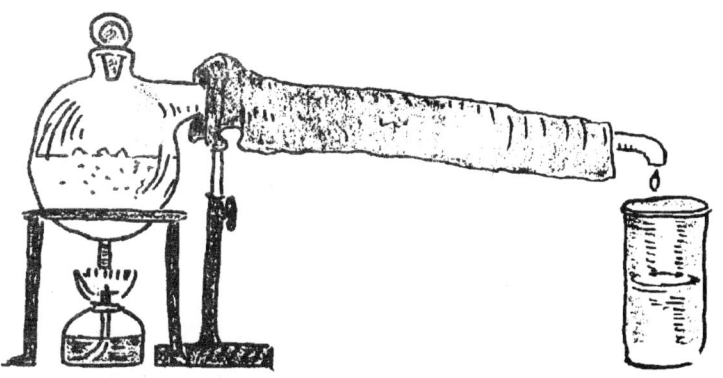

A still with cold water cloth aiding condensation of vapour

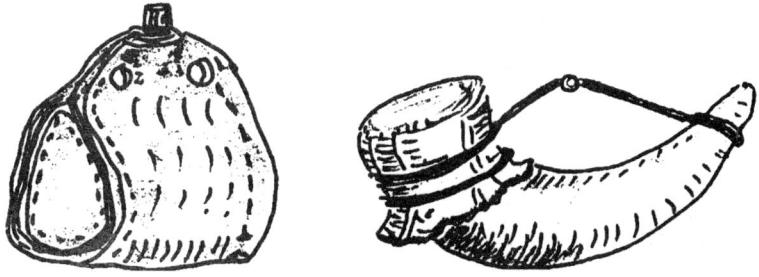

Leather jack and horn – both items were used for storage.

17th century glass bottle. The initial 'S' = Stamford

Break Fast at Bradgate

Bradgate House kitchen, February 1988

The Old House, Hereford, August 1991

Note: rack for spare spits above fire on the chimney breast.

Compare:
(i) with engraving of Elizabethan kitchen,

and

(ii) with Bradgate House kitchen inventory of October 1681.

Break Fast at Bradgate

This view of an *Elizabethan kitchen* shows spit roasting.

Spare spits are kept over the mantlepiece and dripping pans collect all the fat which falls from the rotating roasts.

Ventilated cupboards, wooden trenchers, large pewter plates and candlesticks can also be seen.

The spit appears to be turned by an early form of weighted clockwork.

Bradgate House, kitchen inventory, October 1680

One great spit
One beefe forke
One brass mortar
One ladle of brass
One shredding knife
One iron fire forke
One iron pail
One great brass pot
One little brass pot
One boiler and one girdle kettle
One great broad greater (sic)
One great stew pan for fish with a cover
One broad brimmed pan
Five iron racks
Five skillets
A Jack and Chains

Two knives
Two salt tubbs
Two dripping pans
Two other stew pans
Two saucepans and two covers of brass
Two skimmers

Three frying pans
Three wooden pastry boards

Four cleavers

Six spits
Six stew pans

Break Fast at Bradgate

Above: Peacocks now roam freely close to the ruins of Bradgate House but these are a recent introduction and are not mentioned in the estate accounts.

Below: Red deer and fallow deer are to be found throughout Bradgate Park's 800 acres. They number some 300 on average and were often fed acorns, carrots and turnips to improve their winter diet during the 19th century. Bosworth Park is known to have provided nine bucks and three does to improve the Bradgate stock in 1838.

Extracts from the Bradgate weekly 'Buying In' Account
Purchases listed A - Z for period 1679 - 1682

Items bought and services paid for by the kitchen steward.

		£	s	d
A				
ale	186 bottles	1	3	3
ale (sage ale)	28 bottles		3	8
anchovies	half a pound			10
apothecaries bill	(Dec 15th 1679)		3	11
aquavite	quart 1		2	8
artichokes	6		1	0
B				
bacon	piece 1		1	8
barley to mault	upon the account		9	4
barme	for two weeks		1	10
baskets	2		2	0
basin	1			9
beans	strikes 4		8	0
beef	pieces 6		17	2
beer (strong)	half hogshead		13	4
beer (strong)	bottles 22		2	8
beer glasses	12		6	0
beesoms - bristle	2		1	6
beesoms - flag	4		1	4
beesoms - staff	12		2	0
blood: Physurgeon for letting my Lady's blood			10	0
blue: for washing	½ lb		1	0
blue: see 2 lb starch and ½ lb of blue			1	8
bottles glass: Robert Slingsby	180	1	12	6
brandy	2 quarts		4	0
brawn - one collar	1		11	0
bream	3		1	6
brewing	4 days helping to brew		2	0
brewing Jone Doer 4 times brewing ale			4	0
brewing William Ison	4 days brewing		2	0
bull John Andrews for a bull	1	2	0	0
butter	lbs 43		14	7

21

Purchases listed A - Z for period 1679 - 1682.

		£	s	d
C				
cabbage nets	2			3
calf skins (to make breeches for Kirke)	2		3	4
candles	10 lbs at		4	1
capers	half a pound			9
carting John Ansty	day(s) 1			7
chains and lock : Aron Mottley			2	6
cherries	12 lbs		2	0
cheeses - seven pounds weight	each		8	4
chickens	13		3	10
chopping wood Jacob Litlin	1 day			8
cider	42 bottles		14	0
cloth: linen to make kitchen boy's shirts	10 yrds		6	10
cockles	peck 1			6
cod (north sea)	60 (each)		1	0
cooper - making hoops : days working	16		16	0
corks	144		5	0
colouring (cloth?)	yards 3½		10	0
crab apples children gathering	5		3	4
crab apples stamping 12½ days - men	3		8	4
crayfish dozen	9		1	6
currants	2lbs			10
D				
dogs grease	2lb		1	4
ducks	2			11
E				
eels	32		18	0
eggs	60		2	9
exchanging of 2 pewter dishes and a saucepan			6	0
F				
fat heifer from Mr Benskyn	1 @	3	10	6
fiddler for playing. (May)			2	0
fieldfares	84		7	0

Purchases listed A - Z for period 1679 - 1682.

		£	s	d
fish (cod)	3		9	6
fish (flounders)	20		4	6
fish (herring)	36		2	0
fish (salt	4		4	0
fishing 4 men number of days each	2		5	4
fishing Jacob's boy one day	1			6
flaskett: for the gardener	1		2	0
flaskett: for the dairy maid (shallow basket)	1		1	4
flounders	20		4	6
forks(size unknown)	5		5	0
fruit (raisins)	2 lb			10
fruit (currants)	2 lb			10

G

gardening: John Rower:	6 days digging		4	0
geese	6		5	0
glasses - beer	12		6	0
glasses - crystal	12		6	0
given to a poor man on my Lady's order				6
gritts	4 quarts			6
grouse - cocks	2		3	0

H

hares	2		2	0
hartshorne	1 lb		3	0
haslett	1			8
hatchet	1		1	0
hemp halters	6		1	6
herrings	52		1	10
hops	11 lbs		5	6
humbles(deer entrails)	2		11	0

I

isinglass	1 oz			6
Iceland (fish)	120	(each)		6

Purchases listed A - Z for period 1679 - 1682.

		£	s	d
J				
jam	6 lbs			6
jug	1			9
K				
keys - for the park gates	2		1	8
kitchen work - Widow Dingley	6 days		1	0
knives for the cook	2		1	8
knotts	12			8
L				
lamb joints	3		9	10
larks dozen	3		2	6
lead new				2
lemons	12		3	0
letter - carrying same to Enfield	1			2
lime - strikes	8		4	0
linen to make the kitchen boy's shirts	10 yrds		6	10
lines for the windmill cloths (windmill on John Hill)	2		3	3
linings to make kitchen boys clothes			3	2
liver beasts livers	8		1	4
lobsters	3		4	6
locks	2		1	2
M				
manna	3oz		2	3
marmaricke glasses	12		4	0
marrow bones, 5 pieces of beef & 3 legs			15	8
mault strikes	8		18	8
mault for making	48 quarts	2	8	0
mestlin strikes	5	1	2	6
millwork:swelling the picks:	John Sutton		4	0
mops	2		1	4
mum	1 tearse			
mustard seed quarts	4		2	0
mutton joints	14		16	9

24

Purchases listed A - Z for period 1679 - 1682.

		£	s	d
N				
nails - one thousand four penny nails for the gardener			2	10
nets - Burbridge the netmaker for 5 days + thread			3	0
nets - cabbage nets	3			6
O				
oatmeal - drying oats and making oatmeal			2	4
oats	8 strikes		10	0
oil - trayne	1 bottle			10
oil for the coachman	3 quarts		3	6
oil	1 quart		2	0
oil of sweet almonds (apothecary's bill)			8	5
old beans	4 strikes		10	0
oranges	12		1	6
oysters	1 barrel		4	6
P				
paper (cap)	1 quire		1	0
partridges	6		1	6
peas for the swine	4 strikes		9	0
pepper (white)	1 lb		2	0
pheasants	2		4	0
pike	3		3	0
pig	1		2	6
pigeons	12		1	5
pipes (for smoking) a gross	144		1	2
plover	7		1	9
poplar sap - for the still			4	0
pork	3 pieces		4	6
potatoes			3	0
pots and milk pans for the dairy maid			4	0
powder (2 lbs) and shot (7 lbs)			3	4
powder (blue) for washing			1	0

Purchases listed A - Z for period 1679 - 1682.

		£	s	d
R				
rabbits	16		5	4
ringing the swine - Thomas Shaw				
rakes	@ 3d each			9
raisins	2lb			10
S				
sacke for ye horses - bottles	2		5	0
sacke in the house - bottles	2		5	10
sacke bottles	6		14	0
salmon	1		6	6
salt pecks	3		1	2
sand	1 lb			6
sandwich ale bottle	1			8
saucepan	1		5	0
sausages	5lb		2	1
scuttle	1		1	0
sheep small	1		5	0
sheep skins	4		1	4
shoeing the bay horse				8
shoes - for the kitchen boy	1 pair		2	10
shoes - for the bay horse	4		1	4
soap	6 lb		1	6
spices and fruit			2	2
spice in the kitchen			2	0
starch: half of blue and starch	2 lb		1	8
stockings for My Lady	2 pair		8	0
stockings for the kitchen boy.	1 pair		1	10
stockings for Godfrey			2	6
sugar loaf			1	10
sugar (coarse)	1 lb			4½
sugar (fine)	1 lb			5½
T				
tailor:John Walker for making kitchen boys clothes				10
teal	4		1	8
tench	1		2	0

Purchases listed A - Z for period 1679 - 1682.

			£	s	d
tobacco	½ lb			1	0
treacle - London	½ lb			3	0
trenchers	24			5	6
tripe	3 dishes			1	0
turkeys	2			3	6

V
veal joints	9			8	8
venison pieces	4			12	0
vinegar quarts	4			2	6

W
washing	5 days				6
washing and clipping sheep				1	4
wax and pens for my Lord					6
weeding in the gardens: Widow Dingley 11 days					8
wheat straw Nicholas Tompson:	1 load			7	0
wheat, strikes	2			7	4
white bread:					3
white mault, (*sic*) strikes	8		1	0	0
white pepper	1 lb			2	0
wigeon	1				5
wine - claret	bottles	5		5	10
wine - white	quart	1		1	2
wine - Port(ugal)	bottles	3		3	6
wine - Rhenish	bottles	2		3	4
woodcocks	2				10
writing paper	quire	1			6

Y
yeast (see barme) quantity unknown:				
weekly average			1	0

Break Fast at Bradgate

Although lacking a floor above the kitchen and smaller windows, this sketch might well have been made inside Bradgate House. The baking ovens, vented straight up into the sky on the south side of the slate flagged area, with the large fireplace to the right, offer a glimpse of what one corner of the Bradgate House kitchen may have looked like. In the absence of any obvious water system serving this south-western corner of the house in which were the kitchen, bakery, brewhouse, scullery and laundry, one can only presume that staff were employed to top up water butts located within the service areas throughout the day or that water collected on the roof was brought down into the kitchen to stand in the large cistern as was the case in the old kitchen at Burghley House, Lincolnshire..

Glossary of 17th Century terms appearing in the Bradgate accounts 1679-1681

Anchovies
Small fish, not much bigger than a middle finger, caught in vast numbers in the Mediterranean and pickled for export.

Barme
The froth that forms on top of fermenting malt liquors which is used to leaven bread; sometimes referred to as godesgoode.

Barrel
Cask of liquid – containing 164 litres, approx. 81 cm tall and 66 cm wide – ⅓ of a butt (see below)

Beer
Generally brewed at home but by 1688 there were a number of public brewers who were selling as many as million gallons a year. This is an average of two barrels, each containing 36 gallons or a daily consumption of 1.75 pints for every man, woman and child throughout the country.

Besom
A broom: a brush of twigs or other materials for sweeping. At least three types, bristle, flag and staff were purchased for use by the Bradgate staff during the 1679-1681 period.

Blanch
Pale coloured ingredients such as sugar, white ginger and cinnamon. Once beaten to a fine powder they were sprinkled upon roasted apples, quinces or pears.

Brawn
The flesh of a pig, collared so as to squeeze out much of the fat, boiled and pickled.

Butt
A liquid measure – containing 490 litres – twice the size of a hogshead, see Hogshead and Pipe below).

Glossary

Cheat
Second quality bread made into larger loaves using whole-wheat flour with bran removed.

Claret
Shipped from Bordeaux, this was the most popular wine for use in cookery. A true claret, *Haut Brion*, was the only chateau-bottled wine with which most gentlemen of the 17th century were familiar.

Cocket
A slightly cheaper white bread than Pandemain, or paynemaine, which was the finest quality bread made from flour sifted two or three times. This bread was replaced by top-quality bread called manchets (hand sized breads) around the year 1500.

Coffin
Pies and tarts of all kinds were extremely popular in Elizabethan England. Often the pastry was made with flour, small bits of butter and hot water, or broth. This dough was kneaded into a stiff paste and then shaped to hold a filling without the support of a tin. The coffin was not always eaten. For sweet fillings, the bottom crust was sometimes flavoured with rose water and sugar.

Cubebs
Peppery Javanese spice berries.

Dottard
A decayed tree.

Drawn
Cleaned and gutted.

Faggots
A bundle of twigs or herbs tied together.

Firkin
A cask of liquid – containing 41 litres – a fourth part of a barrel, or seven and a half imperial gallons and in size approx. 53 cm high and 36 cm wide.

Glossary

(N.B. Butter, tallow, fish etc. were sold in barrels called firkins but these were of indeterminate size and capacity).

Flasket
A shallow basket for carrying vegetable produce etc. Purchased at Bradgate for the dairy maid and the gardener.

Food dyes
Black:　from dried blood.
Blue:　from syrup of violets.
Green:　from parsley juice, or spinach.
Orange:　from marigold petals - used as a cheese dye.
Purple:　from the turnsole and heliotrope flowers.
Red:　from alkanet, a red dye from the roots of south European borage.

Galanga
A dried rhizome from China much used in medicine being an aromatic stimulant with a taste very similar to that of ginger.

Grease
Dog's grease was the lowest form of rancid butter. Rancid Irish butter was imported and used for sheep salve.

Gritts
A coarse scouring agent, harsher than sand, used for cleaning pans etc. Some gritts may have been thrown to chickens to encourage birds to lay eggs with strong shells.

Haberden
A large salted cod.

Hartshorn
The antler of a hart or stag. More like normal bone than the horn of an ox. At Bradgate the shavings off the horn would have been used in the kitchen as a jelly stiffener.

Haslet
The entrails of a beast, especially a hogs liver, heart and lights.

Glossary

Hogshead
A cask of liquid – containing 246 litres or 51 gallons – measuring approx. 95 cm tall, and 72 cm wide. Half a butt or 1 hogshead.
(Peculiar to the London area, the term was used to indicate a measure for 63 old wine gallons, 54 of beer and 48 gallons of ale.)

Horse bread
Bread which included peas, beans and any other grain to hand.

Ice Houses (not to be found at Bradgate)
These first appeared in royal palaces in the 1660s thus allowing winter ice to be preserved throughout the year. By the mid 18th century many large houses had similar facilities allowing them to produce ice cool fruit drinks, sherbets, wines and frozen creams during the hottest summer weather.

Isinglass
Derived from the swim bladder of certain fish such as sturgeon. (see picture on page 57)

Kilderkin
Cask of liquid – containing 82 litres – and approx. 65 cm tall by 56 cm wide.

Lamb's Wool
Ale mixed with the pulp of roasted apples.

Leache
Slices.

Malmsey
Originally red or white wine made from grapes grown in a region called Malvasia, near Naples, Italy.

Malt or Mault
Grain, usually barley steeped in water and made to germinate, the starch of the grain being thus converted into saccharine matter, after which it is dried in a kiln, and then used in brewing ale or beer.

Glossary

Manchet
The best white bread "eight ounces into the oven and six ounces out".

Manna
A sweet sugary juice obtained from the stem of a species of ash tree *Fraxinus Ornus* a native of Sicily and other parts of southern Europe. The best manna is in oblong pieces or flakes and is a whitish or pale yellow colour and somewhat transparent. It was used as a gentle laxative and given mainly to children although it could be used in conjunction with other more active medicines.

Marchpane
Marzipan – usually a large disc of almond paste, iced and decorated for special occasions.

Marle
Rosemary.

Marle bone
Marrow bone.

Mestlin (Maslin)
Mixed grain, especially rye mixed with wheat. Term is also used for bread made with mixed corn. (There are numerous variations on the spelling of Mestlin.)

Mum
Brunswick mum, a heady and potent ale matured for two years before drinking. Mum was popular in the late 16th century and in some places special mum houses were opened. Pepys diary records a visit made in 1664 to the 'Fleece', a mum house in Leadenhall.

Pin
Cask of liquid – containing 21 litres – a small barrel shaped container measuring approx. 43 cm high and 36 cm wide.

Glossary

Pipe
A liquid wine measure of 105 imperial gallons. In practice the amount varied depending on the type of wine the pipe contained. Thus port wine was nearly 138 gallons, sherry 130 gallons, Madeira 110 gallons and Lisbon 140 gallons. The 'Pipe' measure was later called the 'Butt'.

Powder douce
Mild spices. Powder douche mixed with saffron was often added to leeks, cabbages and parsnips to give an interesting flavour.

Powder fort
Hot spices such as ginger and pepper.

Ravelled
Bread containing whole-wheat with some bran.

Sacke
A Spanish amber wine usually dry, or very dry but some sweeter types were available and imported in increasing quantities during the late 17th century. Sacke is first mentioned on a wine importation list of 1532.

Sage ale
Herb and spice flavoured ales were still fashionable long after the establishment of plain hopped ales and beers. Two or three drops of the extracted oil of sage with a quart of ale made a very acceptable drink and the same could be done with the oil of nutmeg, mace and the like. In fact with one good butt of ale many changes could be made and guests would wonder how the host was able to come by such a variety of liquor.

Small beer
A light ale usually given to children. Drunk copiously during the summer months by adults avoiding water!

Stockfish
Dried cod – no salt – hard as a board.

Glossary

Strike
A bushel = 4 pecks = 8 gallons.

Tearse
35 gallons or a third of a pipe, liquid measure.

Tent
A deep red wine from Galicia or Malaga, Spain.

Tourte
Known also as brown bread. It contained husk as well as flour and may have been the bread used for trenchers.

Trayne oil
Expressed fish oil, most commonly pilchard. High in vitamin 'D' although this was not realised until this century.

Treacle ale
A light, thin beer made with treacle sweetened water, mixed with barme to produce a kind of ale.

Trenchers
Thick pieces of bread on which food was eaten at table, or on which food might be cut up. Later 'trenchers' became the name of the wooden plates which replaced the slices of bread.

Tun
210 gallons or two pipes.

Turnsole
A purple flower of the heliotrope family used as a medieval food dye.

Verjuice
Made in large amounts at Bradgate. Crab apples fermented to form a sharp kind of vinegar. Used in cooking but mainly used for pickling.

Wastel
Another first-quality bread from well-sifted flour.

Wether
A yearling cow or sheep.

Glossary

Zedoary
A spice root with a ginger taste which is bitter, pungent and a toxic aromatic. From India and China originally.

The large brew house vats have survived at Charlecote House, Warwickshire due to their use long after other large houses had closed down their brew houses and switched to buying in beers and ales.

At Bradgate, in the 17th century, crab apples were collected and it took three men 12½ days to tread them in vats very much like the example above. The resultant sour juice (verjuice) was used for pickling rather than being converted by fermentation into crab apple wine. It is, at first reading, strange to find that the kitchen purchased cider at 3½d a bottle from local merchants when it could easily have been produced in Bradgate's own brew house. It must be remembered, however, that the normal months for brewing were October though to March, since no scientific methods of cooling had been invented, and these months saw the brewing vessels in use entirely for beer and ale, such was the consumption and demand by the household, their friends, visiting tradesmen, the estate servants and even tenants.

Glossary

Charlecote House, Warwickshire c1551 (National Trust). Perhaps the nearest building of similar date and close similarities to Bradgate House. The washhouse and brewhouse at Charlecote contain fixtures and fittings house of mid 18th century date but the original 1550s building remains with only minor alterations to its windows. The brewhouse, laundry boilers and baking oven are all grouped within the building ensuring a concentration of coals, wood and water within a small area not dissimilar to the south-west corner of Bradgate House.

37

Bradgate House Account Book
Page for June 27th 1681

The last week's expenses in the house: the expenses – the value of the remains in the House.

The last week's expenses	The value	The Comings in	Remains in the House
8 Peeces of beefe & 4 pallets	£1 9 4	8 peeces	7 peeces of Beefe
11 Joynts of Mutton	13 6	13 Joynts	3 joynts of Mutton
7 Joynts of Lamb	5 0	8 Joynts	2 joynts of Lamb
8 Joynts of veal & 4 burrs(?)	10 0	2 Joynts	1 joynt of Veal
4 Salt Fishes	4 0	00	34 great eels & 41 Salt Fishes
30 Pound of Butter	12 6	30 & 26 lb	23 stray sheep & 4 lambs
60 Eggs	2 9	28	5 pence in eggs
17 Chickens	4 6	28 Chickens	32 Chickens & 10 Capons
6 Rabbit	2 0	6 Rabbits	2 Rabbits
5 Pounds of Bacon	1 8	00	3 flitches & 17 Pounds Bacon
4 Dishes of Crayfish	3 4	00	14 score & 19 pounds of Soap
2 Bream	4 0	00	28 wether sheep
7 Cheeses wayed 50lb	8 4	6 Cheeses	4 old & 37 New Cheeses
10 pound of candles	4 1	00	12 dozen & 10 pounds of Candles
6 Hogsheads of beer	£1 16 0	16 Hogsheads	20 hogsheads of small beer
2 Strikes 2 pecks of wheat	15 0	1 Strike	1 Strike - 1 Strike wheat
5 Strikes of Mestlin	£1 2 6	2 Strikes	64 strikes & 2 pecks Mestlin
3 Pecks of Salt	1 2		4 strikes & 2 pecks of salt
00 Barme	2 2	00	Score and 6 pounds of hops

38

Bradgate House Account Book
Page for June 27th 1681

4 Quarts of vinegar	2 6	00	9 Staffe beesoms
4 Staffe beesoms	8	12 Beesom	10 bottles of rent wine
6 Pounds of soap	1 6	13 gallons of Brandy and .....(struck out)	
2 Bottles of sacke in the house	5 10	00	5 dozen & 7 bottles of sacke
2 Bottles of sacke for the horses	5 0	3 bottles and 3 bottles of bought sacke	
5 Bottles of claret wine	5 10	18 dozen bottles – 18 dozen bottles of claret	
1 bottle of sandwich ale	8	8 dozen bottles and 1 bottle of sandwich ale	
2 Bottles of Rhenish win	3 4	9 dozen bottles of Rhenish wine	
3 dozen bottles and 6 of cider	14 0	4 dozen bottles & 6 of cider.	
15 dozen & 6 bottles of ale	£1 3 3	22 dozen & 6 bottles - 41 dozen & 4 of ale	
Half a hogshead of strong beer	13 4	00	23 hogsheads & a half of strong beer
00 spice and fruit	2 2	00	2 shillings in spice and fruit
11 pounds of hops	5 6	00	Tearse of Mum
2 pounds of ye course sugar	9	00	Tease of claret
1 pound of ye finer sugar	8	00	A hogshead of wine
1 doz. & 10 bottles of strong beer	2 8		7 dozen and 2 bottles of strong beer
			61 lbs of the best sugar
			66 lb of the courser sug

Sum is £13 8 8

To Mr Cocke from Mr Becher: 12 loaves of double refined sugar, 11 loaves of single refined sugar, a box containing a quarter hundredweight of double refined sugar.

39

Break Fast at Bradgate

In most large houses fresh meat could be kept close at hand by keeping a dovecote or pigeon-house in the house grounds. At Bradgate the dovecote is known to have received attention to its roof by the estate mason, Joseph Sketchley of Anstey, as late as 1787 – nearly fifty years after the abandonment of the main dwelling house.

Bee keeping and the collection of honey to provide a sweetener is thought to have been practised from the late bronze age onwards. However, from comments made by writers during the mid 17th century, it becomes clear that sugar, though expensive, was already beginning to find more favour with cooks. Mead continued to be brewed using honey but gradually even this long established drink dwindled in importance, yielding first to imported sweet wines, and by the 18th century to home-made wines too. As if to confirm these general facts the Bradgate inventory of 1679-1681 makes no mention of honey, hives or bee keeping throughout the whole of the period mentioned and sugar appears to be plentiful.

Bradgate House, Leicestershire
c.1500 - 1739

Few 17th century household papers exist for Bradgate House, Leicestershire. The one small account book that has fortunately survived shows the weekly buying in of foodstuffs, wines, ales and apothecary items. The book also records the issuing of oats for animals and more general household requirements like cleaning materials and cloth. There are also references to small payments made to delivery boys, girls and for other small services. In total the book allows readers some 300 years later a precious view, both inside and outside the grand house, during the period 1679 -1681.

The kitchen inventory drawn up in 1680 reads as follows:

One	boiler and One griddle kettle.
One	brass pot and One broad greater.
One	great stew pan for fish with cover.
One	little brass pot – One iron pale
One	great brass pot.
One	iron fire fork – One great spit
One	shredding knife.
One	ladle of brass.
Two	other stew pans + Two dripping pans.
Two	saucepans + Two covers of brass.
Two	skimmers.
Two	salt tubs and two knives.
Five	skillets and One broad brimmed pan.
Six	stewpans and Fifty brim barons.
Six	spits – One beef fork.
Two	cleavers – One brass mortar
Three	wooden pastry plates.
Three	frying pans – a jack and chains.
Five	iron rakes

Bradgate House c.1500 – 1739

When the Mistress of the pantry at Bradgate, Ruth Hudson took over from the old scullery maid Susanna Carre in October 1680 the following items are mentioned:

One.....................pastry plate.
One ....flat stand.
Two ....cheese plates.
Two ....salts.
Two ....salvers for fruit.(One sent to London and five plates).
Three ....bedpans.
Three ....pair of snuffers.
Four ....brass candle sticks.
Four ....ring stands.
Six ....French plates of a large size.
Twelve...............French plates of a small size.
Eight..................chamber pots.
Nine...................candlesticks.
Twelve...............trenchers.
Twelve...............stew pans.
Twenty-four.......pewter plates.
Fifty...................brim basins.
Ten dozen (120) pewter dishes.

From the number of kitchen utensils listed, it can be seen that the number of people catered for within the house was quite small and would by estimation rarely exceed thirty persons. The daily number requiring meals depended on the number of visitors and, most importantly, whether the Earl of Stamford, the Countess and their attendants were in residence. Due to the issuing of oats for visitors' horses being noted in the account book it can also be seen that rarely did visitors – they are referred to as 'strangers' in the accounts – stay over night at Bradgate and one must presume that if entertaining was to be done it was usually far more convenient for both host and guest(s) if the Earl's London house was used.

Bradgate House c.1500 – 1739

A guide to Casks and Barrels

	Capacity (litres/galls)	Weight empty kilos	Weight full kilos	Height cms	Width max/min cms
Butt	491/108	106	596	132	84/67
Hogshead	246/54	69	314	95	72/61
Barrel	164/36	53	216	81	66/54
½ Hogshead	123/27	45	168	76	62/50
Kilderkin	82/18	34	115	65	56/44
Firkin	41/9	19	60	53	44/36
Pin	21/4.5	12	29	43	36/30

Bradgate House c.1500 – 1739

Stock taking in the various cellars during October 1680 gives a few extra clues about the holding locations of the cider, ales and verjuice. The wine cellar, unfortunately does not have a a stock check.

In Richard Hudson's two cellars:
- 3 Hogsheads of unracked cider.
- 3 Hogsheads, 3 quarts and one tearse of verjuice.

About 45 dozen glass bottles.
- 4 Gross of corks.
- 28 Empty hogsheads.
- 3 Empty butts.
- 1 Butt and One hogshead full of small beer.
- 7 Firkins and 3 covers.
- 3 Hornes.
- 3 Lundishes (?).
- 12 Caffikines (?) and one case.

(Richard is a servant who appears to be in charge of the pantry at this time.)

In the Brewhouse:
- 2 Butts.
- 3 Hogsheads.
  and all the brewing vessels.

In the small beer cellar:
- 5 Hogsheads of small beer.
- 6 Empty firkins.

Bradgate House c.1500 – 1739

In the gardeners' chamber:
- 2   Empty butts.
- 16 Hogsheads (Empty).
- 4   Covers.
- 1   Skip to carry bottles in.
- 2   Jacks.
- 3   Hornes.
- 16 Dozen empty bottles.

In the strong beer cellar:
- 7   Dozen and one bottles of strong beer.
- 15 Hogsheads of strong beer (3690 litres)
- 6   Hogsheads (Empty)
- 3   Hogsheads and a piece of hogshead verjuice
  (Verjuice used for cooking and pickling, rather like cider vinegar.)
- 4   Empty firkins which had sandbich* ale in them.
- 4   Dozen of candles
- 2   Bottles of old ale
- 22 Dozen (264) of new bottled ale
- 1   Firkin of old stale cider

* Sandbich ale has proved impossible to trace. As the word 'sandbich' is sometimes written as 'sandwich', enquiries have been made in the area of Sandwich, Kent but without success. A suggestion has been put forward that that the word may refer to an early 'porter' which is a dark-brown bitter beer made from charred, or browned malt – similar to today's Guinness. If the latter suggestion were correct the Bradgate 'sandbich ale' would pre date 'porter' by some forty years.

Bradgate House c.1500 – 1739

Of the kind of food served before 1700 we know a great deal from other surviving household rolls, the keeping of which became normal practice from at least the 13th century onwards. Those of the Countess of Leicester, dating from 1265 and Sir Thomas Vavasour, Ham House 1610, are amongst the most revealing and often quoted. In addition Samuel Pepys(1633-1703) writings about food eaten and prepared for functions he attended in the 1660s sheds further light on eating habits of the late 17th century

These early lists indicate trends, fashions, variety and the availability of food and drink especially those items newly introduced from the Americas along with tea and spices from the eastern countries. Taken together the indications are that by the late 17th century Bradgate was rather behind what was current and almost commonplace in the metropolis.

The absence of coffee and cocoa – both available in England from 1655 onwards and both very fashionable as drinks and food additives in London is at first a little surprising especially when it is remembered that the Earl and his family made frequent visits to their London house, entertained guests there, and visited in their turn other grand houses both within and close to the city. It must be remembered, however, that coffee, cocoa and tea were very expensive to buy during the 17th century and purchases of this type would not have been made by the kitchen staff at Bradgate. It is far more likely that purchase of a specialised nature would have been made by the Countess or Earl of Stamford himself, and these special items would have been recorded in their own personal account books.

The trenchers mentioned in the items handed over to Suzanna Carre (new scullery maid) in September 1679 were by this time old fashioned and in most upper class houses trenchers had long since been replaced by plates of pewter, silver or gold which could be prominently displayed on open shelves within the dining room.

Bradgate House c.1500 – 1739

Poultry was consumed in enormous quantities, beef and mutton were eaten on the non-feast days of Sunday, Monday, Tuesday and Thursday. The fast-days of Wednesday, Friday and Saturday were at times not strictly followed and it became necessary in 1548 for an Act of Parliament to be passed which reintroduced Saturday as a fish day. Fifteen years later Wednesday was also made a statutory fish day. The humble salted herring was the staple diet on such days and even Henry VIII considered a fresh herring a delicacy. Eggs could be eaten on ordinary fasting days but not in Lent and according to medieval cookery books eggs could not be used in cooking during this period of the year.

During the Commonwealth, fish days were abolished as a Popish institution. However, after the Restoration efforts were made to revive the fish days with the intention of encouraging the fishing industry and at the same time, providing more seamen for the crown in times of war. But by this time, the fish that was available, was both difficult to find and expensive. People who had enjoyed freedom from statutory fish days were, as one might expect, most unwilling to go back to them.

Some items mentioned in the Bradgate accounts have both local and historical significance and therefore require elaboration, a selection of some of these items follows:

Birds

Birds had a two-fold appeal in Britain's diet, firstly they provided fresh meat, especially in winter when so much salted flesh was normally eaten, and secondly because of the variety of species taken for the tables of the rich. The dinners of the nobility and gentry, who kept large households and entertained many guests, were served in two main courses – at the greatest feasts sometimes in three = made up very largely of meat dishes, unless it was a fasting day.

Small birds were seen as a meat delicacy throughout Britain at

Bradgate House c.1500 – 1739

the time the account book was being kept. Larks, blackbirds and fieldfares (winter visitors) in particular, were highly prized and favourites amongst the small birds eaten, and this is reflected in the larder purchases at Bradgate.

Being so small the tiny birds presented special difficulties for the cook when roasted. To avoid the birds drying, or even worse charring, they were tied on to the full sized roasting birds as these cooked on rotating spits. Larks received high commendations from physicians in the 17th century, whilst blackbirds, fieldfares and thrushes were also seen as well worth considering. Sparrows, however, came very low in the gastronomical league table being deemed to be "hard to digest" by nearly all writers who had eaten, and then suffered them !

To catch the larks a Hobby (a small falcon) was used in the sport called 'daring of larks', in other words, petrifying the larks with such fear that they stayed on the ground, where the fowler took them easily by throwing nets over them.

At Bradgate a 'faulkener' (keeper of the falcon(s) appears in the account book. This visitor is recorded as drawing oats for his horse in March 1681. One must assume that this particular faulkener, or falconer as we would call him today, is likely to have been a special visitor invited to put on a display for guests, or a special event. Larks, when not caught by the faulkener, could be purchased locally at thirty pence for three dozen so there was really no need for a full-time faulkener on the staff at this time..

Cooking the small birds.
Recipes of the period suggest that cooks pluck the larks but do not gut them, truss the legs with a leaf of red sage to every lark between the joints of the legs. Then having the yolks of eggs beaten, apply same by dipping a feather in the solution. Smear over the body of each lark and then cover well with crumbs of bread. Have ready thin slices of back bacon about three inches long, and an inch broad. Lay the larks

Bradgate House c.1500 – 1739

in a row side to side, with a piece of this bacon between every two larks. Then pass little spits about twelve inches long through the sides of the larks. Upon each spit, place a piece of bacon so that the outsides of the larks, are shielded for a time from the full heat of the fire. While they are roasting bathe them well with fat from the dripping trays and once cooked serve the birds with the following sauce:-

> *Fry grated bread crisp in butter and having set them before the fire to drain and harden, serve them upon the table upon the spit, by which means they keep hot the longer.*

They may be eaten with the juice of lemon, and with the fried crumbs of bread but some likewise eat them with the gravy sauce which is normally made for a roasted turkey.

Note:
Though the guts are left in the larks – they weree not to be eaten.

Birds in season
Hens were deemed to be good for eating at all times, but perhaps best from November to Lent. Peacocks were rated by most as being good at all times, but when young and of a moderate statue, they could be as good as pheasants. Cygnets were deemed to be best between All Hallowe'en day and Lent. Mallards were rated to be good after a sharp frost, till Candlemas, as were teal and other wild fowl that swimmeth. A woodcock was at its best from October to Lent. Pheasants, partridge and rail were thought to be good in all seasons but best when taken with a hawk. Quail and larks were other birds thought to be always in season, as were pigeons if they were young.

Instead of roasting larks and fieldfares could be cooked in wine with bone marrow, raisins, a little sugar and cinnamon. Another recipe suggests small birds could be boiled in "the best mutton broth" with a little whole mace, whole pepper, claret wine, marigold leaves, barberries, rose-water, verjuice, sugar and marrow, or else sweet butter". "Stockdoves, or teal, pheasant, partridge or such other wild fowls" were simmered in good beefstock with plenty of coleworts (small cabbages).

Bradgate House c.1500 – 1739

Other bird stews were flavoured with fresh barberries or gooseberries; and capons and hens were sometimes boiled with bitter oranges or lemons. These fruity stews continued into the Stuart period (1613 – 1713) often in the form of hashes with mushrooms, chestnuts, anchovies, or oysters, as extra ingredients. During the 18th century, however, the fruit element tended to be discarded. It was possible to pickle larks and a recipe written down in 1727 shows that normally they were boiled and then put in vinegar, well seasoned with herbs, spices and plenty of salt: 'once in a month new boil the pickle – when the bones are dissolved, they are fit to eat; put them in china saucers, and mix with your pickles'.

In the poorer households larks continued to be enjoyed and even sparrow dumplings were not unknown. Blackbirds, thrushes and finches began to lose their appeal during the 18th century. There are still records of song birds which were taken alive on the outskirts of London during the 1770s but these had been caught with the aid of nets and tame decoys, to be sold not as food but as cage-birds. The females, however could not sing, so they were killed off and disposed of at threepence or fourpence a dozen.

As Bradgate House was left to slowly decay in 1739 there were already signs that the small wild birds so frequently featuring in the first or second dinner courses some sixty years previously, were fast falling from favour.

Woodcock *Widgeon*

Bradgate House c.1500 – 1739

A Table of Fowl
The most proper season for the Four Quarters of the Year.

March, April, May
Turkeys with eggs
Pheasants with eggs
Partridges with green eggs
Pullets with eggs
Green Geese
Young Ducklings
Tame Pigeons
Young Pigeons
Young Rabbits
Young Leverets
Caponettes
Chicken Peepers
Young Turkeys
Tame Ducks
Young Rooks
Young Sparrows

June, July, August
Ruffs, Reeves, Godwits
Knotts, Quails, Rayls
Peewits, Dottrells
Pheasants, Polts
Young Partridges
Heath Polts, Black or Red Game
Turkey Caponettes
Flacking Ducks
Wheat Ears
Virgin Pullets
Young Herons
Young Bitterns
Young Bustards
Pea Polts
Wild Pigeons

September, October. November
Wild Ducks
Teals
Wild Geese
Barganders
Brandgeese
Widgeons
Shelldrakes
Cackle Ducks
Cygnets
Pheasants
Partridges
Grouse
Hares
Rabbits
Buntings
Wild Pigeons
Capons
Pullets

December, January, February
Chickens
Woodcocks
Snipes
Larks
Plovers
Curlews
Redshanks
Sea Pheasants
Sea Parrots
Shuflers
Divers
Ox eyes
Pea Cocks and Hens
Bustards
Turkeys
Geese
Blackbirds
Fieldfares, Thrushes

Bradgate House c.1500 – 1739

Butter

Butter intended for cooking purposes was clarified. It was used melted and strained and then put into pots and kept until required. Almond butter could be served at table in place of the more usual kind while olive oil was sometimes bought for fish frying rather than using butter.

In early May butter was prepared for the benefit of children. Writers in the 17th century describe how it was made by setting new, unsalted butter on open platters out in the sun for twelve to fourteen days. This bleached out the colour and much of the vitamin A, and made the butter very rancid. But at the same time it acquired extra vitamin D from exposure to the sun's rays, and thus had some curative power for children with rickets, or pains in the joints known as 'growing pains'.

Ordinary butter was thought to be "good for growing children and for old men in their decline, but very unwholesome betwixt those two ages". Children were therefore allowed to eat butter in Lent but most adults strictly kept the fast and avoided it. One Venetian visitor to England shortly before 1500 noted that children here were given 'bread smeared with butter in the Flemish fashion'.

Butter's oiliness also gave it some value as a laxative. "Some persons have wanted too a fine a diet and have eaten no bread but manchet. They would benefit by eating of brown bread and butter in a morning (which is a countryman's breakfast) and by doing so they will find themselves as soluble as if they had taken some purgation". In producing this effect, the branny bread must have been quite as active as the butter.

At Bradgate butter was either made in the kitchens, was brought to the house by villagers as whole, or part payment of rent, or was purchased from local yeomen farmers. Not all this butter was consumed at Bradgate however, for the account book shows a regular supply of butter – between 7 and 20 lbs a week – being sent down to the Earl of Stamford's London house in the year 1680.

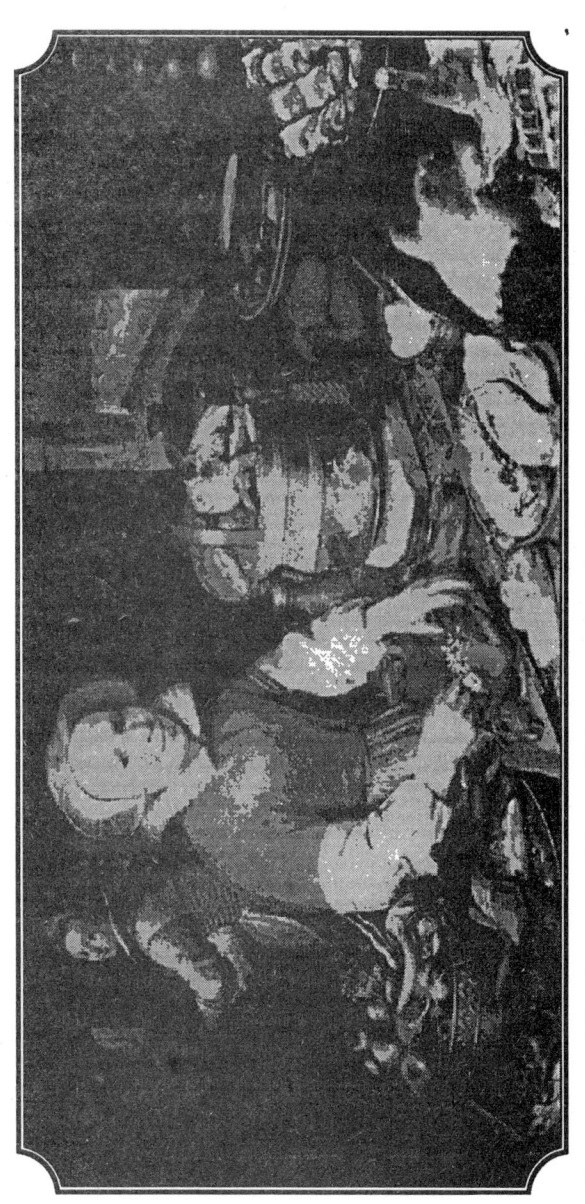

Bradgate House c.1500 – 1739

The range of foods required for a 17th century meal of two courses in a large country house is well portrayed in this Dutch painting. The growing, and continual improvement of vegetables, by the Flemish and Dutch meant that by the early 17th century exported produce was arriving in south-eastern England and before long the gardeners themselves arrived. Market gardening, especially around London, proved lucrative. Gardeners who worked within a six mile radius of London formed themselves into a guild, which obtained a charter in 1605.

Bradgate House c.1500 – 1739

Salt and Fresh water Fish and Eels

A cold pie was a means of preserving fish, for such pies were filled up with clarified butter which when set excluded the air. Medieval rents were sometimes paid in eel pies; and twenty-four herring pies made of the first fresh herrings of the season, each pie containing five herrings flavoured with spices, were rendered annually to the king by the city of Norwich. Fish pies often contained not only spices, but also dried fruit, wine and sugar, all of which made them distinctly sweet to the taste.

One pie that was made to mark the mid-point of Lent had a filling of figs, raisins, apples, and pears, all ground up and cooked with wine and sugar to which was added boiled fish – calver salmon, codling or haddock – with spices which themselves had been pounded with pestle and mortar. The mixture was then placed in its pastry coffin with stoned prunes and quartered dates 'planted'ß on top.

Fish jelly was a favourite feast dish, eaten in the second, or even the third course, that is if the occasion was grand enough to demand three. Tench, pike, eel, turbot and plaice were considered suitable for the purpose. They were cut up and boiled well in wine, or a mixture of wine and vinegar. Then the fish pieces were removed and laid in dishes, while the broth was spiced and coloured with saffron or other dye, further reduced and skimmed. It was strained through a cloth, poured over the fish and left to set.

The 60 firkins of North sea cod and 120 firkins of Island (Iceland) fishes bought by Bradgate House staff at the Stourbridge Fair – the fairground is now a suburb of Cambridge – in 1680 would have been heavily salted and originally landed at Yarmouth before being brought to the Fish Hill, close to the River Cam on the northern edge of the Fair site close to the Newmarket Road.

Fishing in Icelandic waters by east-coast fishermen is thought to have begun in the early 15th century. Two and three-masted

Bradgate House c.1500 – 1739

ketches with rudders, larger and more stable in heavy seas than the smaller boats normally used by east-coast fishermen in home waters were used for these expeditions. These mariners set out in February and March taking with them provisions for the summer and lots of salt. When they reached Icelandic waters they caught cod, gutted it, then salted the fish on board before drying it (the summer climate being too warm and humid for successful wind drying); and at the end of the summer when all their salt had been used and absorbed, they sailed home in time for the autumn fairs and markets.

Not all the fish were salted and dried. Some were barrelled in salt and left in their own pickle until the ship returned to its home port. Fish in this state were known as green fish. Sometimes these fish were taken out and dried at the end of the voyage, after spending several weeks in brine. The degree of hardness and dryness obtained varied with the method of curing.

The smoking of herring seems to have been a development of the 13th century. The fish were first given a long soaking in heavy brine, then strung up and smoked in special chimneys for many hours before finally they were barrelled. The best fish were said to be large, fresh, soft and pliable, well salted with their roes safe inside them. Red herrings were described by writers of the period as having excellent keeping qualities.

At Bradgate there are frequent references to house staff fishing at Groby Pool where carp, chub, bream, tench, perch, roach, dace and pike would have been taken. Eels were to be found in many rivers, especially the Fens. They were also imported from the Netherlands throughout the Middle Ages.

Thirty-four great eels and forty-one salt fishes are recorded amongst the food stocks held at Bradgate in the summer of 1680. Eels were cheaper to buy than most fish, and were probably the only fresh variety, other than shellfish bought by poor people. Freshwater crayfish appear regularly in the accounts and in great numbers, thirty-

Bradgate House c.1500 – 1739

five dozen (420) at 5/10 being recorded for the week ended 30th June 1679.*

During the 17th century potted fish, like potted meat, became a fashionable dish at the tables of the well-to-do, being served among the lighter fare of the second course. Period recipes abound for the potting of eels, lampreys, salmon, smelts, mackerel, lobsters, shrimps and any fish regarded as particularly desirable. Potted fish was to become such a popular method of preserving, that the earlier method of keeping fish by sealing the fish with butter within a cold pie fell almost completely out of favour with the cooks and chefs in the latter years of the 17th century.

Before the discovery of the value of root crops as a winter food, many animals had to be killed off in the autumn simply because there was not enough food to keep them all alive until the following spring. It was impossible, without refrigeration, to keep all this meat sweet through the winter months, and some became noticeably tainted. Thus, the strong spices of the East, red peppers, cloves, ginger, nutmeg, cinnamon, and others were needed to mask the putrid taste of the meat. Originally these spices were brought from the East by camel caravans across the desert. They could only carry articles of small bulk, and whatever they brought was naturally very costly. Spices and sugar were important items of this caravan trade, but were so expensive that they were luxuries that only the rich could afford.

The Bradgate accounts show white pepper being purchased at 2/- (10p) for 1 lb in December 1679 and a 1 lb of black pepper at 1/2 (6p) and Jamaican pepper (sometimes called allspice), 1 lb at 1/1 in the July of the following year.

*There are no references to the Bradgate House fish ponds in the 17th century accounts. These ponds can still be clearly seen on aerial photographs of the house.

Bradgate House c.1500 – 1739

Isinglass

Isinglass is of a firm texture and whitish colour, derived from the swim bladders of certain fish like the sturgeon. The two dried bladders shown here (both over 12 inches long) would be finely ground to produce a gelatin-like substance.

It is used in the preparation of creams and jellies and also used in fining liquors of the fermented kind; in purifying coffee; in the making of mock pearls; stiffening linens, silks, gauzes etc. With brandy it forms a cement for broken porcelain and glass. It is also used to stick together musical instruments and as a glue for binding many other delicate structures.

Isinglass was frequently used in t e Bradgate kitchen usually purchased as a powder.

Bradgate House c.1500 – 1739

New foods are recorded in the rhyme referring to 1520
Turkey, carp, hops and beer,
Came to England all in one year.

Apples and pears were the oldest English fruits and there were established orchards. Foreign fruits, especially oranges and lemons and dried fruits from Portugal, were imported as luxuries. When Edmund Verney of Claydon House, Buckinghamshire, went up to Trinity College, Oxford in 1685, his father wrote:

In your trunk I have put for you
18 Seville Oranges	*1lb of brown sugar candy*
6 Malaga Lemons	*lb of white sugar candy*
3 pounds of Brown Sugar	*1lb of raisins, good for a cough*

1 pound of white powdered . Four nutmegs sugar made up in quarters.

Samuel Pepys (1633-1703) wrote about the food available at the numerous dinner parties and functions he attended in the 1660s. As a Principal Officer of the Navy he had £350 per year to live on and could live comfortably. For such people whose incomes were quite satisfactory, meat was about 3d per pound, bacon 4d, good cheese 2d, draught ale 2d per flagon and bottled ale 6d a dozen.

At one dinner party in 1663 Pepys and his guests sat down to a dinner dressed by his own maid. They had fricassee of rabbits and chicken, leg of boiled mutton, three carp in a dish, a great dish containing a side of lamb, a dish of roasted pigeons, a dish of four lobsters, three tarts, a lamprey pie – a most rare pie – a dish of anchovies, good wine of several sorts. All these things Pepys described as being, "very noble and to my great content.". All of this menu could have been produced at Bradgate for the same meats and fish appear in the Bradgate accounts of 1678-1680.

Pepys travelled with his own set of forks and often noted their absence at other tables*, even at a lord mayor's banquet. Napkins and ewers were normally still used and Pepys noted that the lord mayor

Bradgate House c.1500 – 1739

did not even provide these. Pepys rarely mentions vegetables although there were improved strains introduced from Holland. Covent Garden at this time was no more than a few sheds grouped under trees on the south side of a fashionable square. Pepys makes reference to cabbage, peas, asparagus, onions, and cucumber but he never mentions tomatoes which had originated from South America.

The Bradgate accounts only occasionally mention even the name of a vegetable but vegetables must have been grown and seeds ordered, most probably in a separate account book held by the gardener, Luke Grewcock. Some seeds are listed in the kitchen accounts such as mustard, radish and turnip. Stray items such as cabbage nets, probably for use by the kitchen staff rather than the garden staff - and the mending of same do receive a mention in the kitchen accounts but potatoes at three shillings for an unrecorded quantity and artichokes, six for a 1/- (5p) are rare items in the accounts and must be seen as items not normally grown in the Bradgate gardens.

Tomatoes were viewed somewhat suspiciously by the English being blamed as likely causes of gout and cancer as they were considered to chill the stomach.

* The buying in of table forks is recorded in the 1678-1680 accounts.

Potatoes

There is a single reference to potatoes within the Bradgate accounts and the reference itself tells little of the origin of the potatoes, type and weight of same, these facts are not recorded. However there are certain inferences which can be drawn from the entry. Firstly, potatoes are being bought in and because of this it is unlikely that they were being grown in the kitchen gardens. Secondly this is not an unusual entry for there would be far more detail if this were an unusual purchased item. From this single entry, 'Potatoes – 3/-' we can conclude that potatoes were being used at Bradgate House in 1679 and had

Bradgate House c.1500 – 1739

been used there prior to this date.

From other sources it is known that it was a long time before Virginia potatoes became at all common in England. Through most of the 17th century it is clear from recipes that potatoes were regarded as a speciality food, whether baked in pies or used to garnish rich boiled meats, such as beef, turkeys, capons, chickens and game birds. In most recipes sweet or Virginia potatoes could be used interchangeably, and probably were, since sweet potatoes continued to be well or even better liked than the Virginia ones. It was late in the century before the starch potential of the Virginia potato was recognised, and boiled, mashed potatoes came into occasional use as a foundation for puddings, in place of bread or cereal flour.

Potatoes were also widely suspected of being the cause of gout and cancer and although the Irish adopted this food widely in Ireland, in England it was not until the19th century that potatoes were sown as a crop by farmers here. Previously, if they were grown in numbers, then they were destined for export.

Rabbits

Rabbits appear to have been plentiful both within the park and nearby. The poorest of families or individuals could take on a particular warren and pay their rent in conies(rabbits) rather than cash, as Thomas Whitely did in 1649. His yearly rent being six score couples (120 x 2 or 240 rabbits) Known rabbit warrens were at Hunts Hill (north west corner of the park) Rothley Plain, Groby Lodge Farm, Cliff Hill, Charnwood and the large warren within the park which was located halfway between Cropston village and Bradgate House on the Broadgate, now better known as Causeway Lane.

Bradgate House c.1500 – 1739

Below are the few returns which still survive of the Causeway Lane. or Park warren.

1759	September 12th to February 12th	
	2255 couples at 18d per couple	= £169 2 6
	Expenses	= £ 16 10 2

1759   1939 couples taken between November 10th 1758
and January 29th 1759   = £153 10 1
November 92, 22, 56, 151, 41, 100, 45, 85, 150, 50.
December 38, 34, 130, 43, 15, 21, 16, 52, 110, 50,
      25, 78, 31, 42, 30.
January 50, 50, 50, 31, 51, 22, 25, 30, 44, 21, 20,
      21, 17.   Total 1939

1764	2057 couples (clear money)	= £138 10 3
	Netting and catching costs	= £ 15 15 0
1765	2054 couples (clear money)	= £139 16 0
	Netting and catching	= £ 14 4 11
1766	905 couples (clear money)	= £ 55 19 4
	Netting and catching	= £ 11 18 2
1767	15 couples (clear money)	= £ 64 18 1
	Netting and catching	= £ 11 4 5

1774   Rabbits caught November 29th 36 couples
December 2nd 60 couples Dec 6th 39 couples
December 13   33 couples, Dec 16th 14 couples
December 22nd 8 couples, Dec 23rd 33 couples
December 30th 42 couples = 265 couples at 18d
per couple   = £ 19 17 6
Catching same   = £ 3 14 6

Bradgate House c.1500 – 1739

776 - 1777	November 27th to February 9th 681 couples (clear money)	= £ 41 7 0
1810	Henry Webb 184 couples of rabbits at 2/6d Expenses in catching	= £23 0 0 = £14 19 0
1822	Henry Webb 1500 couples of rabbits at 1/6d and 203 at 9d Expenses in catching	= £120 2 3 = £ 4 10 0
1823	Henry Webb 69 couples of rabbits at 1/6d = Expenses in catching	£6 6 6 = £4 10 0
1828	127 couples summer rabbits 1311 couples winter totals Expenses	= £104 13 6 = £ 33 12 7

Sugars

Of all the items on the medieval spice account, sugar was the one destined to have the greatest effect on Britain's eating habits. For many years the high prices asked for imported sugar caused its value to be seen only as a medicine and it is believed that even the Romans during their occupation of the British Isles only knew sugar as a medicine rather than a food and drink sweetener.

The first sugar refineries are thought to have opened in London in the 1540s and by 1598 even the traditional English drink of unsweetened ale had given way to sugar sweetened beer in the south of England.

A 17th century dinner party wound to a close after meat and pudding, with a banquet laid out to enchant the eye in patterns of glistening, gaily coloured sweetmeats, chief among them the thick

Bradgate House c.1500 – 1739

fruit pastes, known as 'marmalades', and a close second marzipan, or marchpane, a mixture of sugar, nuts, pineapple and almonds made into small, biscuits, or small cakes – all individually shaped and lavishly decorated. Frothed egg whites mixed with essence of almond were also used to form fancy cakes in the form of macaroons and meringues. The whole of this third course must have occupied the Bradgate kitchen staff for a considerable length of time prior to the feast and would largely explain the large amounts of sugar 'in hand' when stocktaking took place at Bradgate.

From the Bradgate House kitchen account book it is known that at the end of June 1681 the inventory of 'remains in the house' record that 12 loaves of double refined sugar, 11 loaves of single refined sugar and a box containing a quarter of a hundred weight of double refined sugar, in addition to 61 lbs of the best sugar and 66 lbs of the coarser sugar was held – the house was quite obviously well prepared to meet the requirements of more than one person with a sweet tooth and Richard Frost, kitchen steward at Bradgate House, was a man carefully topping up already plentiful stocks! Sugar was eaten in large amounts at the court of Elizabeth I (1558-1603) for the queen herself is known to have had almost black teeth in her early twenties.**

The ordinary man and woman had to rely on more natural sweeteners. The most natural of all perhaps being honey. Sugar because of its high price, was for the nobility and gentry, for whom the recipes in the medieval cookery books were composed. In Elizabeth's reign there were many common folk who had never tasted refined cane sugar.

Beer differed from ale in that bitter herbs were added in the-brewing process and sugar was added for strength. For a long time the additional hops and sugar was seen as an adulteration which caused the offices of 'ale connes' or 'ale tasters' to come into being. There are traditional tales of these officials sitting in spilt beer to see if their leather breeches would stick to the wooden bench, or stool, because

Bradgate House c.1500 – 1739

of the high sugar content.

As well as plain sugars of several grades, sugar candy, rose-scented and violet-scented sugars were imported, and those who could afford them (they were more costly than even the finest ordinary sugar) consumed large quantities.

The royal household in 1277 used 677 lbs. of sugar, and also no less than 300 lbs. of violet sugar, and 1,900 lbs. of rose sugar.

Sugar for kitchen use came in several grades, according to the degree of refining which it had undergone. The coarsest was sold in large loaves which could weigh several pounds apiece.

In Leicestershire, the Bradgate House inventory taken June 27th 1681 refers to :- 'Two pounds of coarse sugar at 9d and One pound of fine sugar at 8d'.

Most of the Bradgate House purchases of groceries and spices came from Mr Richard Freeman, a Ratby based grocer and dealer. However, prices could be considerably cheaper if goods were purchased at fairs. There are surviving accounts of bulk purchases made at the 1681 Stourbridge Fair, Cambridgeshire by the Bradgate House staff. These show that Mr. Freeman's prices could easily be bettered if really large amounts were purchased, as is the case when bulk buying even today. The added cost of employing a carter prepared to move over a ton of goods from Stourbridge to Bradgate still made this yearly bulk purchasing excursion worthwhile.

The carter charged £1 6s 8d for moving the goods and whilst all the goods are not listed, those that are show that: 115 lbs of fine sugar was purchased at 5d per pound and 113 lbs of coarse sugar was bought at 4d per pound. (One hundredweight = 112 lbs, or sometimes shown as 1 cwt).

***The Englishman's Food,* J.G. Drummond and Anne Wilbraham.

Bradgate House c.1500 – 1739

Tea (absent from the kitchen accounts at Bradgate)

Tea was first brought to England from China by the Dutch East India merchants in 1658 and until the early 18th century it was to remain both a scarce and expensive commodity. Its absence from the ordinary kitchen accounts at Bradgate is not unusual during this period in history, for such an expensive item. Initially the price of tea was three pounds and ten shillings (£3 10s) per pound. Soon afterwards the price dropped to £2 0 0 and then £1 0 0 a pound and in the coffee and chocolate houses of this time it was served as a weak infusion without milk.

The Earl and Countess of Stamford would have been well acquainted with the new and fashionable drinks being served in the London coffee houses as they frequently entertained guests at their London house, 37 Charles Street, during the 1670s and '80's. Such an expensive item as tea would have been purchased by the Earl, or more likely the Countess of Stamford and kept within a lockable caddie within her private rooms. Both the Earl and Countess would have had their own personal account books – known from other records seen – and their London house would have proved a valuable place to exchange gossip on where and how to make the best purchases of the new drinks such as tea, coffee and chocolate, all of which were highly fashionable diversions at this time.

Of the three drinks, tea soon became the most popular.

In 1700   20,000 lbs of tea was imported.
In 1710   5,000,000 lbs of tea was imported.
In 1800   20,000,000 lbs of tea was imported.

So, by 1800, tea had replaced beer as the universal drink of the poor. Another calculation has indicated that out of an income of £40 per year in the 1790s an average family would spend £2 0 0 on tea and sugar.

Bradgate House c.1500 – 1739

Venison

Venison is a very dry meat. There is practically no fat on some joints, so rinds taken off ham, or bacon pieces have to be wrapped around the venison whilst cooking. The salty rind of bacon will cause the venison to redden but this is not harmful to the meat, in fact it sharpens the meat's flavour. Venison takes longer to cook than most meat and must on no account be taken too early from the cooking vessel otherwise it will be tough. The best results are to be obtained by using a skewer. When it goes into the thickest part easily the meat is cooked. Venison should never be served with thick brown gravy. It should be served with any juice that comes from the meat plus a glass of red wine. This will ensure that the gravy is clear and bright.

Wines and Spirits

Aqua Vitae

Aqua vitae was neat spirit, generally distilled in the still-room at home by Tudor and Stuart housewives (the physician Thomas Cogan reckoned, in *The Haven of Healtyh*, 1584, that it took a gallon of strong ale or wine to produce a quart of 'reasonable good aqua vitae'). A rough country marc or brandy will do nicely, though for a Christmas party it might be wise either to dilute this sweet and exceedingly potent drink with liberal amounts of hot water, as for a nineteenth-century punch, or to reduce the proportion of spirits from equal parts to one part per four or five parts red wine. Heat the alcohol gently with the sugar until it is dissolved, before adding the spices. Crushed 'whight pep' or white peppercorns give a delicious aroma (so long as you avoid the ready-powdered variety which will almost inevitably be stale); the ginger which was to be sliced "in greate peeces" means green ginger root, and it should be peeled first; the hard, dry nutmegs sold nowadays are more easily grated than cut up, though this can be done with a small, strong, sharp knife. Add a blade or two of mace if you can, adjusting all quantities to suit your taste. The dried petals of 'red jeyllyflowers', or clove carnations,

Bradgate House c.1500 – 1739

commonly used to 'give good couloure' to alcoholic drinks, make a pretty but inessential addition.

For special occasions a wine sauce reinforced with aqua vitae was poured over the pottage in dishes, set alight with a wax candle and served flaming.

In the early days of distilling, wine or wine-lees were the usual source-materials. When the distillation contained enough alcohol to burn, it was called aqua ardens or aqua vitae. A stronger spirit, produced by repeated distilling was known as the quintessence. The 16th century saw the emergence of a rival to wine in the form of spirits. In 1527 the first English translation of a continental manual for distillers, Hieronymus Braunschweig's *The Vertuose Boke of Distyllacion*, was published, and English versions of other similar books followed. They contained descriptions of apparatus, as well as recipes for the extraction of alcohol from wine and the waters from herbs, flowers and fruits.

Those in the distilling trade used wine-lees and broken wines (obtained cheaply from vintners and coopers) to produce aqua vitae which, as a result, was often very crude. To conceal the nauseous flavour of the raw spirit they added aromatic herbs and spices and these in turn gave their supposed medicinal properties to the drink. *Aqua composita* was a name often given to such concoctions. Dr Steven's water and rosa solis (confected with large amounts of that herb) were two which found great favour in Tudor and Stuart times. All such warming drinks stimulated the action of the heart, and they became known as 'cordial waters'

Tent Wine

The name 'Tent' is now extinct but it was an English name applied to dark red wines from the coastal zone near Cadiz, especially from the town of Rota. Tent appears on cellar wine lists from the Middle Ages

Bradgate House c.1500 – 1739

up to the middle years of the 19th century.

Tent, called by the Spanish, tintilla, or tinta di Rota, was described as a rich wine drank generally drunk after dinner. The 'rent' wine mentioned in the Bradgate accounts was this wine. Ten bottles of 'tent' wine are mentioned in the stock-taking of the Bradgate cellar stocks on March 18th 1680 – Lady Day the 25th March was a rent day

In the 1830s tintilla had about 13.3 degrees of alcohol, no more than a modern burgundy. In all probability the grapes were those known to the French as 'Teinturiers' whose juice is as red as their skin. Samuel Pepys had a small cask in his cellar and it appears on Victorian menus in the 1860s. Why the name died out is not clear for it was a completely English name for a dark red wine and one would perhaps expect the name to be transferred to 'claret'. For it then would have been directly comparable to, and complementary with claret, or even a dark red wine such as the Spanish Duero.
Note: see also Sacke in Glossary (p. 34)

Cleaning agents
Sand
The buying in of sand regularly features amongst the Bradgate kitchen and household purchases. Floors and stairs were kept clean with sand. It soaked up the grease droppings, as well as mud and dirt trampled in from the outside, an even distribution being obtained by means of a sieve. Sand was also used for scouring metals.

Robert Plot, in *The Natural History of Oxfordshire* (1677), noted that the finest sand dug in the parish of Kingham was used for scouring pewter "for which purpose it so very excellent, that the retailers sell it for a penny a pound".

Sand could also be used, in conjunction with ground oyster shell, for imparting a gleam to brass, for cleaning china, or more prosaically, to remove food adhering to the bottoms of cooking utensils.

Bradgate House c.1500 – 1739

In Cornwall where sand was freely available, housewives scoured their pots and pans (as well as bedroom floors) with 'gaird' or 'growder', which was the local granite reduced to powder. Steel was usually polished with emery paper or, like brass, with white brick, a calcareous earth moulded in the form of a brick, made at Bridgewater in Somerset. Silver and plate were cleaned with white clay, or 'whiting' as it was called. If the silver was particularly tarnished it was washed in lye – water made alkaline with vegetable ashes.

Lye
Lye was made out of fern ashes – especially in the rough and heathy districts where these were plentiful and wood in short supply. People collected ferns while still green, round about harvest time in July or August, half-dried them in small heaps in the open air, and burned them into fine reddish-grey ashes, usually in pots – hence the word 'pot ash'. The ashes were then made into balls of about 3 inches diameter (with the help of warm water) and sold at a penny a dozen. In Newtown Linford, Swithland and within Bradgate Park itself ash balls were made so that everyone had enough for washing and scouring the whole year round and any extra stock could be sold for a little extra pocket money.

Soap
Soap was expensive to buy yet it could be collected or made for nothing. However, the animal fats or vegetable oils that went into its making were also required for other purposes, such as cooking and candle making; indeed, the demand for these items was so great that additional supplies were already being imported from abroad in the late 17th century. To make matters worse soap was subject to substantial excise duties periodically from 1643 to 1853.

Bradgate House c.1500 – 1739

Pock Marks

To take away the pock-holes or any spot in the face:-
Take white rose-water, and wet a fine cloth therein, and set it all night to freeze, and then lay it upon your face till it be dry. Also take three poppies, the reddest you can get, and quarter them, taking out the garbage. Then still them in a quart of new milk of a red cow, and with the water thereof wash your face.

Poplar Sap

Poplars for to still – Bradgate House account book July 7th 1679. Gerard's *Herball* (1597) claims sap of the white poplar tree makes a fine contraceptive: "the same bark is also reputed to make a woman barren, if it be drunke with the kidney of a Mule".

Lighting

Now that electric lighting is commonplace for everyone at the flick of a switch, it takes an imaginative step backwards into the dark to appreciate how much time and effort the Bradgate staff had to spend on providing themselves with artificial illumination. For, although most of the house would take advantage of natural light by rising with the sun, few wanted to go to bed at dusk. This was the time of day when they wanted to gather round the fire and relax and the pipes and tobacco mentioned in the accounts were very probably passed around.

Except in mid summer, all households had to have some form of artificial lighting in the evenings. Those who economised by relying solely on the flickering rays of their fires, were considered mean and contemptible and were often the butt of jokes.

Existing documents show that in 1696 there were only eighteen 'glass houses' or factories making window glass in England and Wales. So it may be seen that only a few wealthy families could afford to live in light and airy houses. The peasantry for the most part lived in windowless hovels, with only a hole in the roof, slits in the

Bradgate House c.1500 – 1739

wall, and a doorway for ventilation and illumination. Although the use of window glass was to rise steadily (a window tax levied from 1696 to 1851 brought the Treasury much revenue), windows remained a luxury until the end of the 18th century. All types of artificial illumination prior to electricity were both ineffective and dangerous: they required everybody's vigilant attention if they were not to cause fires, the latter being a very common occurrence. Of the 4,413 fires that broke out in London between 1833 and 1849 investigators thought that 2,876 (or 65%) were the result of accidents with candles.

One of the most common types of lighting devices to be found in many of the inland areas of England, Wales and Ireland until the late 19th century was the rushlight, or rush candle. This was a small blinking taper, made by stripping a rush, except for one small strip of bark which held the pith together. The rush was then dipped in tallow. Its light was extremely feeble, but it had the advantage of being cheap and easy to make.

The scummings of the bacon pot, any kind of whatever fat, and bee's wax, mutton suet mixed with grease were all recommended – a rushlight required little attention once it was lit. A well made specimen, 28 inches long burned for 57 minutes, a smaller one 15 inches long lasted for about 30 minutes. All that was required was to move the rush light up when it had burned down to its holder, a job usually performed by children, "Mend the light" or "mend the rush" was an instruction that they all knew well.

Candles, rather than rushlights were used in large numbers at Bradgate but whilst being a more mobile form of lighting than the rushlight (four shillings for 10 lbs in 1679), they were certainly more expensive than rushlights. Tallow candles were also far more trouble to maintain for their wicks were only partly consumed in the course of burning and had to be 'snuffed', pinched or cut off, at frequent intervals if they were to remain bright. (No references to rushes in the accounts at Bradgate).

Bradgate House c.1500 – 1739

On many small islands off the British mainland and in many coastal areas, families burned fish oil lamps. The local fishermen would land their catch, cut out the largest fish livers, store them until they were rancid, then boil them to extract the oil.

The Bradgate accounts show that oil was purchased weekly by the quart but it is doubtful if this small amount of oil was used for lighting, especially if one uses the early 19th century oil requirements of Belvoir Castle as a guide. Belvoir, when occupied, required six hundred gallons of oil to maintain four hundred lamps during a sixteen to seventeen week period.

Water

The main water supply for Bradgate House was by way of a carefully engineered leat and dam across the river Lin close to what is now called Little Matlock near the Newtown Linford entrance to the park.

The leat runs for a considerable distance across the park before entering the walled gardens under a section of walling carried on a bridge. The water is then channelled into a holding pond or reservoir, which remains full of water to this day and can still be seen on the northen side of the house ruins. The water, surplus to house requirements, was ducted towards the eastern side of the house where, as the channel left the walled gardens in the south-eastern corner, it provided a a head of water which drove the Bradgate watermill. From here the water returned to the river Lin after passing through the dog kennels which during the 16-18th centuries stood just south-east of the mill.

There are references in the 17th century accounts which mention the replacement of an old lead cistern which contained some 15 tons of lead. This may mean that the kitchen area had a holding tank of water, or what is more likely, this is a reference to just one cistern used for the collection of rain water from the roof drains. As lead topped, pointed towers, feature strongly in drawings showing the south-western corner of the house – where brewhouse, kitchen,

Bradgate House c.1500 – 1739

scullery and stillroom were located – it is likely that the rain water collected was piped into these working areas from the tower cisterns. Fish ponds, also located close to the reservoir now remain only in outline. From the 17th century onwards, there are references to fishing expeditions being made by Bradgate staff, to Groby Pool and Thurmaston Mills. These were the main areas where freshwater fish were taken on a regular cycle and one must presume almost immediate consumption for only salted fish show in the returns of 'remains in hand'.

The Country Wedding, a painting by Peter Bruegel (1530-1569)
The rent day dinner held twice a year at Groby Old Hall,
for Bradgate tenants, would not have looked unlike this scene.

Bradgate House c.1500 – 1739

References:
Many books have been consulted and many inaccuracies concerning dates and the availability of certain foods noted. Thankfully C. Anne Wilson's book was read at an early stage and proved to be the most reliable source book of all the books listed below.

Food and Drink in Britain – From Stone Age to recent times. C. Anne Wilson, 641.3, Constable & Co. Ltd., ISBN 0 094560 40 4.
Subsequently reprinted by Penquin Books in 1976 and 1984.
ISBN 0 140465 46 4.

C. Anne Wilson worked in the Brotherton Library at the University of Leeds, and her interest in the history of food was aroused when she catalogued Mr. John F. Presto's collection of English Cookery Books, ranging from 1584 to 1861 when these books were presented to the library in 1962.

Great Cooks and their Recipes – From Taillevent to Escoffier. Anne Willan, Pavilion Books Ltd, 1992.
ISBN 1 851455 96 5.

The Cookery of England. Elizabeth Ayrton, pp. 547, Penguin Books, 1977.
ISBN 0 140468 19 6.

The English, A Social History 1066 - 1945, Christopher Hibbert, pp.784, Grafton Books, 1987.

Abandonment of Bradgate House

In November 1739 the 3rd Earl of Stamford died. His son, also called Henry Grey succeeded his father to the title and it would seem that the new 4th Earl made an almost immediate decision to vacate Bradgate House and continue the improvements which had been started at Enville Hall – the stables at Enville are almost certainly of this period. At the same time over at Bradgate the account books record that the doorways and windows had been bricked up in and around the house and sheep had been purchased to graze the former 22 acres of walled gardens by Christmas 1739.

Being over 200 years old and seemingly without major improvements to its fixtures and fabric at this time, Bradgate House was almost certainly lacking in fashionable features like piped wholesome spring water – indications are that the river Lin still provided the main water supply by way of a leat entering the rear of the house. Rain water collected in one or more large lead cisterns probably provided the only other source of water within the house.

The third Earl of Stamford, Harry Grey, had improved Enville Hall in Staffordshire to such an extent that water powered spits had been installed in the kitchen there and were very much talked of in the surrounding area. Bradgate House, some sixty years on from the latter date, probably required expensive repairs and refurbishment, for since the 2nd Earl's death in 1720 (he is buried in the chapel at Bradgate) there would have been little use for the house itself. Even when William III visited Bradgate in the summer of 1696 the improvements that had been made were largely superficial, and in the case of the stables – additional stabling had been hastily thrown up before the king's arrival – very short lived afterwards judging by the earliest surviving map of Bradgate House and park c.1746.

75

ASHBY CASTLE

The Bradgate House list of servants c.1680 can only be partially reconstructed by using the kitchen accounts 1679-1681. However within the pages of John Nichols, *History and Antiquities of Leicestershire – West Goscote*, there is a Check Roll of servants working at Ashby Castle during August 1609. The staffing levels at Ashby Castle appear quite similar to Bradgate House so it would appear that direct comparisons can be made between the two locations.

Check Roll of servants at Ashby Castle – August 1609

Mr Harvey	- Steward
Mr Devinport and Mr Kerrey	- Gentleman Ushers.
Mr Wright	- Clerk of the Kitchen
....	- Gentleman of the Horse
Michael Baughtye	- Yeoman of the Horse
John Burrows and John Holland	- Yeoman Ushers
Raph Goodwin	- Head Cook
Richard Burke	- Under Cook
John Judson	- Usher of the Hall
Davyd Parry	- Yeoman of the Cellar
George Tompson	- Yeoman of the Butterie
Thomas Wallis	- Yeoman of the Pantry
Thomas Masham	- Yeoman of the Wardrop
Edward Hibbard	- Baker
Richard Kinsey	- Brewer
John Dutton	- Yeoman of the Granarie & Porter
Robert Midleton	- Almoner
George Flynthurst	- Seweller (Waiter - bringer of meats to the table)
Thomas Bishop	- Slaughterman
Robert Mantle	- Sculleryman

Ashby Castle

Thomas Lawkin and John Yates	- Scullions
Thomas Wright Senior & Junior	- Gardeners
Fadarra & David	- Footmen
Edward Foster	- Faulkner
Thomas Poyner	- Mr Kerry's man
Thomas Blaze	- Mr Chetwin's man
William Faulkner	- The Faulkner's man
George Wilson	- The Huntsman's boy
Henry Armeston	- The boy of the stable
Henry Ford	- The coachman's boy

These two have their meat in the house – Henry Butler and Richard Vincent

Old Nurse Hoogh	Weaver
Edward Audytor	Thomas Chicken
Mrs Fisher	Mrs Clavers - Gentlewomen
Margaret Watts	Elizabeth Weever - Chambermaids
Nurse Sheepy	Nurse Jomson
Sara Daubney	to attend the children
Elizabeth Butler	Launder - Maid
Elizabeth Clarie	Launder - Maid
Ruth Middleton	Launder - Maid

Number of my servants, both men and women are 61

The number of my gentlemen = 4

The number that dine and sup daily besides strangers and others that come from out of town, are 68

The Bradgate Kitchen Account Book, 1679–1681

Introduction

The following pages have been selected from the accounts as a good example of an average week's activities in and around the house.

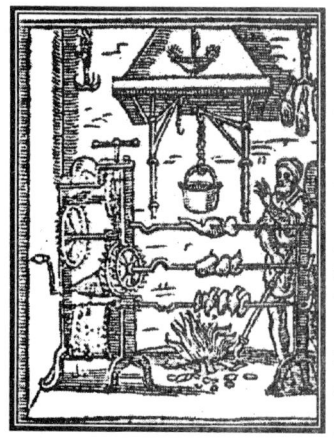

Each page records different events as well as the continuous inflow of foodstuffs and other items necessary to sustain such a large house and staff. Although this was a period in history well after Elizabeth I had died (1603) not a great deal had changed in the daily pattern of life at Bradgate. Oranges and lemons were now more plentiful, sugar and spice appear to be expensive but readily available and the charge for carrying a letter to Enfield, in Middlesex, was surprisingly cheap at 2 pence (January 5th 1678).

The Countess was obviously unwell, the Earl frequently writing letters. The washing and clipping of the park sheep caused one lamb to escape to Cropston much to the delight of the finder as the reward for returning the lamb was two shillings and six pence – as good as a week's wages.

The kitchen boys needed shoes, stockings and shirts; a cooper was summoned to prepare new casks and the brewing cycle was continuous. The water mill needed attention, the laundry was running short of starch and blue, and the new gardener, Luke Grewcock was busy with John Rower – when the latter was not helping with the brewing – and two women weeding the gardens.

Thomas Grey, 2nd Earl of Stamford was not happy with the rule of Charles II and in 1683 – two years after the last entries were made within the account book – Bradgate House was searched for arms after an attempt on the King's life.

Account Book

July 7th 1679
Payed to Richard Frost his bill for the last weeks layings out at markets and of his other payments and disbursments as following :-   £   s   d

for 6 peeces of beefe..		7	2
for 15 joynts of Mutton...1		0	2
for 3 joynts of Lamb..		2	0
for 3 joynts of veale...		8	6
for 12 chickens...		3	8
for 4 quarts* vinegar...		2	6
for 2 quarts of Oyle...		4	0
for wax and penns for my lord..............................			6
for 12 Staffe beesoms...		2	0
paid George Randle for 8 strikes of lime...............		4	0
paid the high Constable for jayle and quartage for year....		5	0
for 8 strikes** of white mault............................1		5	0
for a strike of wheat...		5	0
for 5 forkes..		5	0
for poplars for to still..		4	0
for a quart of Aquavite......................................		2	8
for the charges of a stray lamb from Charley.......		1	2
paid Robert Slingsby for 15 dozen of bottles........1		12	6
paid Mr Freeman a bill for fruite and sugar.........		3	8
paid Kinton for bringing from Lester (carrier).....			6
for 8 strikes of oates..		10	0
for the Physurgeon for letting My Lady's bloud....		10	0
given a poore man by My Ladyes Order...............			6
paid John Ansty for one day getting up wood.......			8
paid John Rower for a day at the same work........			8
for 26 pound of butter......................................		8	8
for eggs..		1	8
for barme...		1	0
for shooeing the bay horse................................			10
for white bread...			3
for 15 dozen of Crayfish...................................		2	6
paid Widow Dingley for weeding 3 days.............		1	0
for charges..		1	0
The **Sum of**	£ 9	12	0

* A **quart** = 2 pints or a quarter of a gallon.
** A **strike** = a measure of the best quality.

79

Account Book

July 14th 1679
Paid to Richard Frost his last weeks bill as here after following:-

	£	s	d
for 6 pieces of beefe		17	0
for 9 joynts of mutton		11	4
for 3 joynts lambe		9	10
for 12 pound of cherryes		2	0
for 3 rakes			9
paid Burbridge the Netmaker for 5 days, mending the (rabbit) nets and thread		3	0
for 2 house locks and for mending other locks and for a chain & nayles		6	2
for a gross of corkes		5	0
for 6 pound of jam			6
for 6 lemons		1	0
for washing and clipping the sheep		1	4
for 2 mopps		1	4
the cooper for two days worke		2	0
paid John Rower for 4 days helping to brew		2	0
Thomas Shaw and Randle for one day getting up wood		1	4
paid Mr Freemans bill for sugar and spice		9	11
paid the Apothecaryes bill		1	4
for 8 pound of butter		2	8
for eggs		2	6
for charges		1	0
The Sum of	**£4**	**4**	**4**

Account Book

July 21st 1679.
Paid to Richard Frost his last week's bill.   **£   s   d**

for 6 pieces of beefe..	16	6
for 9 joynts of veale...	8	8
for 9 joynts of mutton..	11	4
for 13 chickens..	3	10
for 2 quarts of brandy..	4	0
for 4 strikes of beans...	8	0
for grosse of corkes...	2	6
for barme for two weeks..	1	10
paid Widow Dingley for 11 days weeding.....................	3	8
for 12 marmaricke* glasses...	4	0
for 7 pound of shot and 2 pound of powder.................	3	4
paid Robert Shaw for 1 day getting up wood................		8
for shooing the bay horse..		8
paid Mr Freemans bill for a sugar loafe etc...................	9	4
for 6 pound of cherryes which Mr Butt bought.............	3	0
for charges...	1	0
for 9 pound of butter to Mr Read of Newtown..............	3	0

The Sum of £ 4   9   2

* Glass experts consulted over the word 'marmaricke' can offer no description of same. However, the first five letters 'marma' are thought likely to refer to some sort of wide brimmed sweetmeat container rather than a drinking glass.

Account Book

December 15th 1679.
Payed to Richard Frost the particulars of his last weeks bill as following :-

	£	s	d
for 6 pieces of beefe and five legs		19	0
for 12 joynts of mutton		13	10
for 6 joynts of veale and two views(?)		6	8
for a haslett			8
for 6 lemons		1	6
for 4 strikes of wheate		15	4
for 6 strikes of salt		9	6
for 4 strikes of peas for the swine		9	4
for 6 pounds of jam			6
for 10 yards of linen cloth to make the kitchen boy shirts		6	10
for linings to make the same boys clothes		3	2
for 3 quarts of oil for the coachman		3	6
paid Mr Freemans bill for spice etc		4	1
paid Apothecaryes bill		3	11
paid Mr Wood for exchange of pewter and mending 5 candle sticks		8	0
for 2 cabbage nets			3
for 23 lb of butter		7	8
for eggs		4	6
for barme			8
for John Ansty for one day going to cart			7
for Thomas Shaw for ringing the swine			6
paid John Dower for 5 days in the garden		2	11
for charges		1	0

The Sum of £ 6 10 5

Account Book

December 22nd 1679

Payed to Richard Frost the particulars of his last weeks bill :-

	£	s	d
for 5 peeces of beefe		15	0
for 14 joynts of Mutton		16	0
for 5 joynts of veale		6	0
for 13 chickens		4	6
for 6 partridges		1	6
for 2 woodcocks			10
for exchanging of 2 pewter dyshes and a saucepan		6	0
for 3 gross of corkes		7	6
for 2 bristell beesoms		1	6
for 4 flag beesoms		1	4
for 12 staffe beesoms*		2	0
for a payer of shoes for ye kitchen boy		2	10
for a payer of stockings for ye same boy		1	10
for 4 quarts of mustard seed		2	0
for the Cooper 4 days work		4	0
for 8 strikes of white Mault	1	0	0
for 4 strikes of old beanes		10	0
for 6 strikes of pease for the swine		4	0
for charge of a stray lambe from Cropston		2	6
for 6 pound of sand			6
paid John Rower for 6 days work		3	6
paid John Ansty for 3 days goeing to cart		1	9
paid Harry Ansty for 4 days helping to brew		2	0
for 21 pound of butter		7	0
for egg		5	0
paid for barme		1	4
for charges		1	0
The sum of	**7**	**1**	**5**

* **Besoms** = brooms made from thin branches bound around a stout handle.

Account Book

December 29th 1679

	£	s	d
the particulars of his last weeks bill as follows:-			
paid to Mr Benskyn for a fat heifer	3	10	6
for 16 joynts of mutton		18	4
for 7 joynts of veale		7	0
paid the Mercers bills for fruit and spice*	1	14	2
for a collar of brawn		11	0
paid for 12 lemons		3	0
paid for 12 beer glasses		6	0
paid for a gross (144) pipes		1	2
paid Aron Mottley for locks		2	6
paid for 2 keys for the park gates		1	8
paid Joan Rower for 4 times brewing ale		4	0
paid for 4 quarts of vinegar		2	6
paid for a bottle of tryne oyle**			10
paid for 2 ounces of Isinglass		1	0
paid for a jug			9
paid for 12 strike of oats		13	0
paid for a quire of writing paper			6
paid for 6 pound of sand			6
paid for two woodcocks			10
paid for 2 strike of pease for the swine		4	6
paid for 16 pound of butter		5	4
paid for eggs		3	6
paid William Ison for one day clearing wood			10½
paid John Rower for one day and a half			10
paid for 10 chickens		3	4
paid for barm		1	0
for charges		1	0
The Sum of	**£ 9**	**19**	**7½**

* A mercer was a dealer in wares, commodities and textile fabrics epecially silks, linens, cottons, etc. Here the word is used in connection with items bought from a dealer in fruit and spices and for mercer read 'grocer', possibly Richard Freeman of Ratby.

** Trayne oil – a fish oil. Usually produced from the blubber or fat of whales, or the expressed oil from pilchards.

Account Book

January 5th 1680

paid Richard Frost for his last weeks bill:-

	£	s	d
paid for 2 peeces of beef and one leg		5	8
paid for 8 joynts of Mutton		10	6
paid for 12 joynts of veale		14	10
paid for 4 hens		2	0
paid upon the account for barley to mault		9	4
paid for 2 strikes of wheate		7	4
paid John Sutton for sharpening and swelling Mill picks		4	0
paid for 24 trenchers		5	6
paid for a gross (144) of Corkes		2	6
paid for 6 pound of sand			6
paid for a pound of white pepper		2	0
paid for 6 pound of starch		2	0
paid for half A pound of powder blue		1	0
paid for 43 pound of butter		14	7
paid for Eggs		4	6
paid Mr Freemans bill		2	6
paid for 6 hempe halters		1	6
paid for 6 Lemons		1	6
paid for a queare of writing pape			6
paid for a queare of Cap paper		1	0
paid for 1000 foure penny Nayles		2	10
paid for carrying A letter to Enfield			2
paid for 4 strikes of pease for ye swine		9	0
paid William Ison for 2 days work		1	5
paid John Rower for 2 days and a half in ye gardens		1	5
paid for barm		1	0
for charges		1	0

The Sum of £ 5 10 1

Account Book

April 19th 1680

	£	s	d
the particulars of his last weeks bill as follows:-			
paid for 5 peeces of beefe 3 legs and 2 Marrowbones..........		15	8
for 17 Joynts of Mutton 1	1	6
for 6 Joynts of veael, 1 head and a view............................		7	8
for one peece of porke		1	8
paid Mr Cradock for wine and ale		10	4
paid Mr Brookesby for sugar and spice..................................		2	6
paid the Apothecaryes bill		4	9
for 2 strikes of wheate		6	4
for 24 pigeons		2	8
for 2 pound of Dogs Grease..		1	4
for 4 quarts of vinegar		2	6
for a gross of pipes...		1	2
for A bason			9
for a quire of paper			6
for 8 strikes of mault..		18	8
paid the high Constable for bread for ye prison		2	3
for 3 yards and A half of cloath for Leonard....................		7	0
for 6 pound of Jam			6
paid Expences about the Tax and for a warrant.....................		3	0
for 18 chickens..		5	1
for A pig...		3	4
for a quart of Oyle		2	0
paid for 12 oranges		1	6
for 15 pound of butter...		5	0
for Eggs...		3	6
paid 3 men for fishing 1 day a peece		2	0
paid Jacob Littlin for 1 day Croping wood............................			8
paid John Rower for 4 days in the Garden		2	8
for barme..		1	2
paid 2 weomen for weeding 2 days a peece		1	04
paid John Ansty for one days at Cart.....................................			8
for charges		1	0

The Sum of £ 6 10 8

Account Book

April 26th 1680
the particulars of this last weeks bill as follows:-   £   s   d

for 5 peeces of beef and one legg		17	4
for 16 Joynts of Mutton	1	1	6
for 5 Joynts of lambe		4	6
for 9 Joynts of veale		2	6
for 12 Oranges and 6 Lemons		2	6
for Colouring 3 yards and A half of Cloth(?)			10
for 2 quarts of Oyle		4	0
for 4 quarts of vinegar		2	6
for 14 Chickens		3	8
for half a pound of London Treacle		3	0
for new lead			2
paid Mr Freemans bill for sugar etc		5	2
paid for clotting* Thorney Close. Little Dumple, Hopyard Meadow Wadleys Meadow, ye Lodge Yard and orchard		10	6
for white bread			2
for 2 loads of wheate straw		14	0
for Ale when we fish at Grooby Poole		1	0
for 8 strikes of mault		18	8
for 6 pound Jam			6
for 4 new shooes for the bay horse		1	4
paid for 4 strikes of beanes		10	0
paid for 4 strikes of wheate		12	8
paid 4 men for fishing 2 days a peece		5	4
paid Jacobs boy for 1 day fishing			6
paid John Rower for 6 days in the Gardens		4	0
for barme		1	0
for 16 pounds of butter		5	4
for eggs		4	6
paid 2 women for weeding 5 days a peece		3	4
for drying Oates and making Oatemeale		2	4
for 9 dozen of crayfish		1	6
for charge		1	0
for 4 quarts of Gritts			6
The Sum of £	**8**	**1**	**10**

* Clotting: raking animal droppings into the earth to improve the grass growth

Account Book

May 17th 1680

Paid to Richard Frost the particulars of his last weeks bill:- £ s d

for 7 peeces of beef, 1 leg and 2 marrowbones	1	3	9
for 16 Joynts of mutton		19	0
for 11 Joynts of Lambe		8	0
for 14 Joynts of veale and one head		15	8
for 12 pigeons		1	5
for 25 Oranges and Lemons		3	6
paid Mr Brookesbyes bill for sugar and fruits		5	7
for 2 payre of shoes for Kirke and Dingley		6	2
for 2 payer of Stockings for them boys		3	8
for 12 pound of sand		1	0
for 30 Chickens		8	9
for 6 Geese		3	4
for 2 Calfe Skins to make Kirke breeches of		3	4
for 4 sheep skins that John Glover had		1	4
Given to Mr Palmers man when he brought the pigeons		2	0
for 4 strikes of old beans		10	0
paid the fidler for playing		2	0
for 2 basketts and 1 scuttle		2	0
for 8 strikes of mault		18	8
for 2 Ducks			11
for 2 Knives for the Cooke		1	8
for 12 Staffe beesoms		2	0
for barme for 2 weeks		2	0
for 31 pound of butter		10	4
for Eggs		4	6
for 16 rabbits		5	4
for 2 strikes of wheate		6	0
for Charges		1	0
paid Leonard Kirke for work done about ye house		2	2
paid John Rower for 6 days digging in the Gardens		4	0
paid 2 women for weeding 6 days a peece		4	0

The Sum of £ 9 4 9

Account Book

May 24th 1680
Paid to Richard Frost the particulars of his last weeks bill as follows:-

	£	s	d
for 5 peeces of beefe		13	0
for 14 Joynts of Mutton		16	9
for 3 Joynts of Lambe		2	0
for 7 Joynts of veale		6	4
for 12 Oranges and Lemons		1	9
for 1 ounce of Isinglass			6
for 30 Chickens		7	8
for a quart of Oyle		2	0
for 4 quarts of vinegar		2	6
for 2 strikes of beanes		5	0
for a quire of writing paper			6
for 2 pound of starch and half a pound of blue		1	8
for 16 pound of butter		5	4
paid Stephen Johnson A day's worke at Grooby Mill		1	0
for Eggs		1	0
for barme			10
paid John Rower for 3 days digging in the Gardens		2	0
paid 2 women for weeding 2 days A peece		2	0
for charges		1	0
The Sum of £	**3**	**12**	**10**

Account Book

May 31st 1680
Paid the particulars of Richard Frosts bill follows: £ s d

for 4 peeces of beefe		11	4
for 13 Joynts of Mutton		17	8
for 10 Joynts of veale		10	6
for 9 Joynts of Lambe		6	6
for A pound of hartshorne		3	0
paid Mr Freemans bill for fruite and spice		6	6
for 12 Oranges and Lemons		1	9
for a quart of Oyle		2	0
for 20 Chickens		5	6
for a saucepan		5	0
for 2 basketts		2	0
for 2 locks		1	2
for shooing the bay horse			4
for a strike of beanes		2	6
for a strike of wheate		6	0
paid Edward Fletcher for 2 loads of wheate		14	0
paid Nicholas Tompson for one lode of wheate straw		7	0
for 8 strikes of white mault		18	8
for 21 pound of butte		7	0
for Eggs		3	0
paid William Ison for 4 days brewing		2	0
for barme		1	6
paid John Rower for 6 days in the Gardens		4	0
paid John Littlin for 3 days worke		2	0
paid 2 women for weeding 6 days a peece		4	0
for 11 quarts and 1 pint of sacke	1	6	2
for 2 Glass bottles			6
for a quart of white wine		1	2
paid for 4 quarts of vinegar		2	6
for charges		1	0

The Sum of £ 8 16 3

Account Book

October 14th 1680

	£	s	d
Paid Richard Frost's last weeks bill as follows:-			
for 5 peeces of beefe 1 Leg and 4 marrowbones		11	8
for 3 Joynts of Mutton		2	8
for 9 Joynts of Veale		5	2
for half a pound of Anchovies			10
for half a pound of Capers			9
for stockings for Godfrey		2	6
for 3 peeces of pork		4	6
for 8 beasts livers		1	4
for a pig		2	6
for 3 dozen of Larks		2	6
Given to Chapmans daughter when she brought chickens		1	0
for 6 bottles of sacke		14	0
paid John Sutton for Millworke		2	4
paid a leavy for Grooby Mills for the year		1	0
for a quart of Oyle		2	0
for 4 quarts of vinegar		2	8
for a strike of beans		2	6
paid for a hatchett		1	0
for 2 strikes of wheate		7	4
for 18 strikes of mault		18	0
for 6 pounds of Jam			6
for 22 chickens		6	4
for 16 pound of butter		5	4
for Eggs		5	6
for barme		1	2
paid John Rower for 7 days gathering Crabbs (apples)		4	8
paid 5 children for gathering and picking Crabbs		3	4
paid 3 men for stamping crabbs 12 days and a half		8	4
paid John Rower for 6 days digging		4	0
paid Widow Hews for 6 days weeding		2	0
paid Widow Borrows for formering (?) a fole at Belton	1	6	0
paid the cooper for 16 days making hoops		16	0
for charges		1	0
paid Jacobs wife for 5 days washing		2	6
paid Widow Dingley for 6 days in the kitchen		1	0

The Sum of £ 8 18 11

INDEX

A
abandonment 4,6,12,74
account book 38, 39,78,91
ale 21, 36
anchovies 21, 58
Anstey 5,13, 40
apothecaries bill 21
aquavite 21, 66
artichokes 4, 21,29
Ashby 12
Ashby Castle (staff) 76, 77
B
bacon 21
bakery 28
barley 21
barme (yeast) 21, 27, 29
barrels 29, 43
basin 21
baskets 21
bay horse 5
be(e)soms 21, 29
beans 21
bee keeping 40
beef 21
beer (glasses) 3, 21
beer (strong) 3, 21, 36
beer 3, 29
Belvoir Castle 72
birds 4, 47, 49, 50
blue (washing) 21
bottles (glass) 17, 21
bracken 6
Bradgate House
  abandonment 4, 6
Bradgate/'Broadgate' 12
brandy 21
brawn 29
brewhouse 44
brewing 21, 39
bull 21
Burghley House, Lincs.28
butt 29, 43
butter 5, 21, 52
C
cabbage 59
cabbage nets 21
calf skins 21
candles 21, 71

candlesticks 42
capers 21
carpenters 10, 11
carting 21
Causeway Lane, Cropston 12, 60
cellar 7, 44
chains 21
Charlecote House 36, 37
Charnwood 12
cheat 30
cheese 21
Cheshire 7
chickens 21
chopping wood 21
cider 21, 39
cider 21, 39
cistern 11,14,72
claret 30
Cliff Hill 60
cocket 30
cockles 3, 22
cod 22, 23
coffee (absence of) 46
coffin 30
colouring 22
Commonwealth 47
cooking (small birds) 48
cooper 22
corks 22
Cossington 12
cows 5, 6,7
crab apples 22, 39
crayfish 22, 55
Cropston 12, 60
cubebs 30
cucumber 59
currants 22, 23
D
dairymaids 5, 7
deer 7, 20
deer barns 12
distilling 67
dogs 6
dog's grease 22
dottard 30
dovecote 3, 40
Dowry 13

drawn 30
drinking water 6
ducks 22
Dutch (vegetables) 5:
E
Earl of Stamford 14
eels 22
eggs 22
Elizabeth I 63
errands 5
exchanging dishes 22
excursions 5
F
faggots 30
fast days 1, 47
fat heifer 22
fern 6
fern ashes 69
Ferrers 13
fiddler 22
fieldfares 22
fireplace 28
firkin 30, 43
fish (cod) 23
fish (flounder) 23
fish (pike) 25
fish (saltwater) 54 -56
fish 1
fish (herring) 23
fishing 23
flaskets 5, 23, 31
food dyes 31
forks 23,58
fowl – table of 51
French plates 42
fresh food 1
freshwater fish 4, 54
fruit (currants) 23
fruit (raisins) 23
G
galanga 31
gardener 1,4,11,59
gardening 23
gardeners chamber 45
gardens 1, 5
geese 23
glass (ale) 16
glass (beer) 16, 23

Index

glass (crystal) 23
glass (wine) 16
grease 31
Groby Pool 4, 73
Groby Lodge 7
Groby 13
grouse cocks 23
guests (strangers) 42
Guinness 45
gritts 23, 31

H
haberden 31
half-hogshead 43
hares 23
harteshorne 23, 31
haslett 23, 31
hatchet 23
hemp halters 23
Henry VIII 47
herbs 3
herring 23
Hinckley 4
hogshead 32, 43
hops 3, 23
horn 17
horse bread 32
horses 5
household rolls 46
humbles (deer entrails) 23
Hunts Hill 60

I
Iceland 23
Ice house 32
inventory (kitchen) 19
Irish 60
isinglass 23, 57

J
jam 24
Johnson family 11
joisting 14
jug 24

K
keys (park gates) 24
Kiddiar Nicholas (map) 12
kilderkin 32, 43
kitchen (irons & spits) 18
kitchen (Bradgate)12,18, 28

kitchen (inventory) 41
kitchen (staff) 5
kitchen (work) 24
knives (for the cook) 24
knotts 24

L
labourers (female) 2
lamb (joints) 24
lamb's wool 32
larks 24
laundry 7, 28
leache 32
lead 11
lead (new) 24
leat 72
leather jack 17
Leicester Castle 11
Leicester – Countess of 46
Leicestershire 7
lemons 24, 58
Lent 47
letter to Enfield 24
lime 24
linen 24
lines for windmill 24
linings 24
lighting 70
liver 24
lobsters 24
locks 21, 24
Loftus Lunds 14
London 7, 46
lye 69

M
malmsey 32
manchet 33
manna 24, 33
map 1746 (John Kiddiar) 15
marchpane 33
markets 1, 4
Markfield 12
marle 33
marle bone 33
marmalade 16, 63
marmaricke glasses 24
marrow bones 24
Martin John 7

Martin Mr. 13
Martin William 7, 14
marzipan 63
maslin 33
mault 24, 32
mead 40
mestlin 24
millwork 24
mops 24
mum 24, 33
mustard seed 24
mutton joints 24

N
Newtown Linford 1, 5
Nottinghamshire 7
nails 11, 25
nets (rabbit) 25
nets (cabbage) 25
new foods 58
nutmegs 58

O
oatmeal 25
oats 5, 25
oil (for the coachman) 25
oil (sweet almonds) 25
oil trayne 25
old beans 25
Old Hall, Groby 13
onions 59
oranges 25, 58
orchard 11
oysters 3, 25

P
paddock 12
paper 25
partridges 6, 25
peacock 20
pease for the swine 25
Pepys Samuel 46, 58
pepper 25
pheasants 25
pigeons 3,6, 25, 40, 58
pigs 5, 25
pike (fish) 25
pin 33, 43
pipe 34
pipes (smoking) 25
plover 25

93

Index

ponds [fish] 12
poor man (begging) 23
pock marks 70
poplar sap 25, 70
pork 25
porter 45
potatoes 4, 25, 59, 60
pots & pans 25
poultry 5, 47
powder & shot 25
powder (blue) 25
powder (douche) 34
powder (fort) 34
pullets 6
R
rabbits 26, 60-62
raisins 23, 28, 58
rakes 26
references 75
rent 4
ring stands 42
ringing the swine 26
root crops 56, 44
Rothley 12, 60
routeways 12
rushlights 71
S
sack (bottles) 26, 34
sack (horses) 26, 34
sage ale 34
sandwich ale 26, 45
salt 26
salted fish 3
sand 68, 69
sausages 26
sea food 1
scullery inventory 42
scullery maids 42
scuttle 26
servants 8, 9, 10
sheep 5, 6, 7, 26
shoes (bay horse) 26
shoes (kitchen boy) 26
spices 56
Staffordshire 7
strangers (visitors) 42
soap 69
still 17

storage containers 17
small beer 34, 44
stockings 26
stock fish 34
stock taking day 38, 39
Stourbridge Fair 1, 2
strike 35
strong beer (cellar) 45
suckets 16
sugar 2, 16, 26, 62-64
sugar (brown) 58
swans 6
sweetmeats 16
swine 6
T
tailor 26
teal 26
tench 26
tearse 35
tent wine 35, 67-68
Thurmaston 4, 73
tobacco 27
tourte 35
trayne oil 35
treacle 27
trenchers 27, 46
tripe 27
tun 35
turkeys 27
turnsole 35
V
Vavasour, Sir Thomas 46
veal 27
vegetables 4
venison 27, 66
verjuice 2, 27
vinegar 2, 27
W
warren 60
washing 7
water 11, 28, 72
wastel 5
wax 27
weeding 27
wether 35
wheat 7
wheat straw 27
white bread 27

white pepper 27
William III
Williams (Colonel) 14
wine 27, 66
wine (crab apple)
wine (tent)
Y
yeast (barme) 27
Z
Zedonay 36

Bradgate and its villages
A TIME LINE... OLD JOHN

This is the introductory volume for the series of books entitled *Bradgate and its Villages* by David Ramsey.

The first part – the 'Time Line' of dates – links events of national importance with those affecting Bradgate Estate from the 11th to 20th centuries.

'Old John' brings us up to the present-day with the reason for the building of the tower by the Earl of Stamford.

An ideal introduction for everyone, who is interested in knowing more than the Lady Jane Grey connection with Bradgate House.

First published April 1996

ISBN 1 898884 05 6   46 pp

also in this series:

Book 3
Was There A Village Called Bradgate?

Draws on both State Papers and archive of documents still held by the descendants of the Marquis's of Dorset 1465-1554, later the Earls of Stamford 1628-1976.

The Broadgate from which Bradgate derives its name still exists. The settlements which at one time became established along its length and took the name 'Broadgate' or 'Bradgate' have now all disappeared without trace – or have they?

and

Book 4
Newtown Linford Notes & The Leicestershire Slate Industry

Takes a close look at the early slate industry within Newtown and Groby Parishes and how the early Newtown settlers slowly developed the land and houses along Main Street. How Charnwood Forest was cut back from the rear of the village in the 1780s and how the waste houses of the poor were incorporated into the village proper. It is hard to imagine now that some of the most expensive houses in the parish of Newtown began as simple, single room dwellings. Improvements slowly stopped the rain, wind and snow from gaining entry to the dwellings but never the numbing cold of the bleak 18th century winters or the frequent visitations made by the plague.